Rogue
Planet

Scott Skipper

Dedication

Dedicated to the late Stephen Hawking
who warned us not to trifle with
artificial intelligence.

ROGUE PLANET

CHAPTER 1

Pan-STARRS noticed it first. They quickly handed it to the Keck group on Mauna Kea who sent an email to the Jet Propulsion Lab in Pasadena. JPL dispatched Margot Medina, astrophysicist, to Hawaii to report on Keck's findings.

She left the Hilo airport in a rented ten-year-old Range Rover with bald tires and began the climb up the switchbacks to the telescopes. At ninety-two hundred feet, she was obliged to spend half an hour acclimating to the altitude. The staff at the visitor center, who saw astronomers frequently, were unimpressed with her credentials.

"Do you have any photographs of it?" she asked an Hawaiian woman in a park ranger uniform.

"No, but we have souvenir postcards."

Margot felt her brow wrinkle in an involuntary scowl. "I wasn't really looking for souvenirs."

"Maybe some nice chocolate-covered macadamia nuts."

"Thanks, no."

"You do have a winter coat, don't you?"

"I'm from California. All I've got is this jacket."

"You better hope somebody will loan you a coat. There's no heat in those domes."

"I'll be all right."

Above the tree line, the sky was that deep, brilliant blue of pristine air, and it darkened as the sun sank behind the peak of the fourteen-thousand-foot mountain. There were patches of snow around the big white domes. She parked close to the doors of the low building between the telescopes.

Inside she found no one to greet her and was uncertain what to do. After wandering in the dark for a time, she found a door marked Keck I. When she passed through it, a man's voice said, "Who's there?"

"Margot from JPL."

"JPL? Oh, Cynthia must have invited you. Close the door. You're letting heat in here."

"Oh, sorry." She let the door closer glide the door shut.

The disembodied voice said, "I'm Vic, Victor Cruz—call me Vic."

"Glad to meet you, Vic. Are you watching the thing?"

He laughed. "The thing, as you refer to it, is all anyone's watching these days—that is, besides the Russians' blockade of Warsaw. Come on up and have a look."

She climbed a short ladder and met the body behind the voice. The image on the big circular monitor was a field of stars. "Which one is it?"

He tapped one innocuous point of light. "That's it."

"It doesn't look like much yet."

"Well, it's still two years out. Still, we're able to estimate it to be a little bigger than the Earth."

"Can you tell what its trajectory will be?"

"It's above the planetary plane, but when it gets closer, the sun will deflect it. We think it will pass inside the orbit of Mars."

"Wow." She cocked her head. "NASA would be nuts not to send a probe to it."

"I quite agree, but there's no telling what NASA might do. They could well be nuts, or more accurately, Congress would be nuts."

"Well, that's a given. Anything else you can tell about it?"

"Still too far away. All we know is it's a rogue planet heading our way. No way to know where it came from or how it got detached from its star."

"You don't happen to have a spare coat, do you?"

"Ha," he laughed, "yeah, we keep a couple for when thin-blooded Californians come visiting." He picked up a phone, punched a couple of buttons, and said, "Cynthia, your physicist from JPL is here, and she wants to borrow a coat." He paused. "Okay." After ending the call, he said, "Go to the opposite end of the admin building—last office on your left."

Cynthia Norwood turned out to be a tall, broad-shouldered woman with shoulder-length dishwater blond hair. "Ah, you must be Margot Medina," she said when Margot stepped into the open doorway.

"Yes, and I want to thank you for inviting me."

"No problem. We need to get more heads thinking about this thing. Oh, let me get you that coat." She opened a locker and took out a dark khaki-colored parka and gave it to Margot.

"Thanks. I should have had sense enough to buy one before I left—not that stores in Pasadena would have them in stock this time of year."

"Yeah, it seems ironic packing a winter coat to come to Hawaii."

"Yeah, there's that." Margot shrugged the coat over her shoulders. It was way too big and had threadbare patches on the elbows.

Cynthia gestured to a laptop on her desk. "Let me show you what we've got." She tapped on the monitor and a model of the solar system appeared. "We spotted it as soon as it got close enough to reflect sunlight. It was simple to spot it moving across the field of stars. By measuring the percentage of light it blocked in passing known stars we were able to estimate its size."

"Vic said it's bigger than Earth."

"That's right. We think it's between nine and ten thousand miles in diameter." She tapped the screen again. "This is what we think it's going to do."

A circle approached the solar system from interstellar space. It was angling downward from above the planetary plane. The orbits of eight planets were shown. *Evidently, Keck people are Pluto deniers,* Margot thought. "Vic also said it would pass inside the orbit of Mars."

She tapped the screen, the circle stopped. "Yes, it will cross the planetary plane here a little over two years from now. At that time, Mars will be on the opposite side of the sun, but Earth will be here."

"It's going to pass damn close to us."

"That's right. We'll be able to get some great images here and from Hubble too."

"Images hell, we should land on it."

"I agree, but Keck doesn't have rockets."

"Well, I know somebody who does."

"I was hoping you would say that," Cynthia said.

Margot rubbed her hands together and blew on them before sticking them into the parka's pockets where she found gloves and a half-eaten candy bar. "What happens after our close encounter?"

"That's a little hard to predict. It will be accelerating, of course, and the sun will bend its course. Exactly *how much* is hard to predict."

"Any chance of the sun capturing it?"

"That's not going to happen, nor will it affect the Earth's orbit."

"That's good to know."

Cynthia touched the screen again, and the circle passed below the planetary plane turning toward the sun but not falling into it.

Margot spent more time with Victor watching the indistinct spot of light not really doing anything. Well before dawn, the power failed.

"Out of diesel again," Vic said. "We won't get another delivery until Friday—if we're lucky."

"Shortages?"

"That's right."

It was still the dead of night when she returned the coat and pointed her Range Rover down the mountain. She had to slow to a crawl when she passed through the cloud layer, and there was a trace of light in the east as she exited the car into the warm, moist air of sea level. Inside the Hilo Hilton, she hung the 'do not disturb' sign on the door and crawled between the sheets.

Margot played hooky for a day and went to Captain Cook's Beach to bask a little in the two-piece bathing suit she bought for the occasion. Later, at the Hilton, she treated herself to the sushi bar and was hit on by two Chinese businessmen from Oahu. She let them buy her a Kirin but left them disappointed at the end of the evening.

She flew home late the following morning and arrived at LAX too late to go to work. Thursday morning, she commandeered a golf cart to transverse the rambling campus of the Jet Propulsion Lab. Her target was a group of offices used by the perpetual squad of visitors from NASA. On entering the boiler room, she paused to scan for a target. NASA people wore distinctive badges. She spotted one alone at a desk reading a report.

"Excuse me. I'm Margot Medina." She offered a business card.

He rose and reached across the desk to shake hands. "I'm Earl Wilding. It's a pleasure." He smiled lecherously.

She ignored it. "Can I have a word with you?"

"Of course. Have a seat."

The visitor's chair was at the end of the desk. He resumed his seat as Margot settled onto the plain gray institutional chair.

"What can I do for you?" he asked.

"I've just come from the Keck Observatory where they let me have a look at the rogue planet."

"Really? That must have been cool."

"It was freezing actually."

"Yeah, I'll bet it was. What does it look like?"

"Not much—just a spot of light, but they say it's going to pass inside the orbit of Mars."

"Whoa, I hadn't heard that."

"Yeah, and Earth will be pretty close at the time, so I was wondering what NASA is planning to do about it."

"That's above my pay grade I'm afraid."

"Is your pay grade high enough to know who I should talk to?"

He rocked back in the swivel chair. "I suppose anybody in the director's office could help you. I wouldn't think that kind of a mission would be classified."

"No, I'd think you'd want to shout that from the rooftops. Any chance you've got a phone number?"

He took his phone from his jacket pocket and scrolled on the screen. "Here you go." He turned the phone toward her.

She wrote the DC number on the back of a business card. "Thanks."

"You free for lunch?"

"It isn't even nine o'clock."

"I did mean later."

Margot eyed the guy judgmentally. He was okay looking for a NASA guy. "I'll let you take me to Sartori's if you take off the NASA badge."

He laughed. "Deal. I'll call you at twelve."

"Make it eleven-thirty. They fill up fast."

"How far is it?"

"It's on Union—not far."

"Great. See you then."

She took the phone number and went to her own office where she placed a call to the office of the director of NASA. It was lunchtime in Washington.

"Shit," she said aloud. At ten-thirty—she figured they wouldn't return from lunch promptly—she called again. "I'd like to talk to somebody about upcoming missions, please."

"May I say who's calling?"

"Margot Medina from JPL."

"One moment please."

A man's voice came on the line. "Sam Grant. How can I help you?"

"I'm interested in upcoming missions—specifically to intercept the rogue planet."

"Oh, yes, the rogue planet everyone is excited about. I'm afraid we have no plans relating to that."

"You've got to be kidding. This is a once-in-a-lifetime opportunity."

"I'm sorry, ma'am, but our budget is projected out five years. We've only got funding for a couple lifts to the Space Station."

Margot shook her head in disbelief. "Crap, couldn't you redirect some funds?"

"That would take an act of Congress, and I'm sure you know what that's like."

"Oh, yeah. Well, I'm disappointed. I suppose the Chinese will tell us about it."

"But probably not much."

"Right. Well, thanks for your time."

She hung up and tried to focus on routine work, which lulled her into a trance-like state. When Earl called, she snapped awake. She met him in the parking lot and guided him to Sartori's on Union. They climbed the stairs and stepped around a homeless vagrant on the landing. Margot asked the hostess for a patio table. She ordered Chianti, he had a beer.

Margot waited until her wine arrived before unloading. "Your useless agency has no plans to launch a mission to the rogue planet. I can't believe it."

"You must know how bureaucratic they are."

"Yeah, but... This is a once-in-a-lifetime opportunity."

"Maybe you'd get a better answer from the Space Force."

"Well, maybe but I don't see any military application in this."

"It wouldn't hurt to call."

"I suppose. You got a number?"

"Not this time. I'm sure you can find them online. Actually, you do know who builds NASA's boosters?"

"Yeah. You're thinking SpaceX might launch their own mission?"

"What's to stop them?"

CHAPTER 2

After finishing her Greek salad, Margot said, "Come on, Earl. I need to get back to my office."

"What's the hurry? I thought we'd have another drink and get to know each other."

"Maybe another time. I've got some calls to make."

Earl's car had scarcely stopped rolling as she leaned across the seat, gave him a chaste peck on the cheek, and bolted from the passenger door. At her computer, she quickly found a number for SpaceX's headquarters in Hawthorne. The receptionist directed her to their public relations liaison, Louis Jansen. Yes, he had time and would be happy to receive her. After a quick stop in the ladies' room, she was heading south on 110 in moderately heavy traffic. It became very heavy crossing Los Angeles and was stop-and-go after she merged onto the 105. The number of cars abandoned on the shoulder seemed to get worse every time she went somewhere.

Jansen met her in the lobby, they exchanged cards, and he offered a tour of the assembly area, which she eagerly accepted.

In the huge hangar, he said, "These are the Falcon boosters and Dragon cargo capsules."

"Are they capable of carrying a crew?" she asked wishing she had done some research.

"To the Space Station and Earth orbit. The really sexy stuff—the Starship—is being built in Texas."

She decided to get to the point. "What I'm really interested in is seeing if you intend to rendezvous with the rogue planet since NASA isn't."

"Let's go to my office where it's a little quieter." His office looked more like a first-class lounge in an airport. When they were seated in a conversation group, he said, "Is JPL planning on building a rover?"

"I haven't heard that conversation, but I'm of the opinion that we should send a manned mission."

"I get it. That's not JPL's thing, and the boys in Florida aren't interested."

"It's more like the boys in Washington aren't interested. I was told it's not in their budget."

"And you're thinking SpaceX should step up to the plate."

She gave him her most persuasive smile. "I don't see how you can resist."

"I'm just the PR guy. That decision would have to come from somebody named Musk. Fortunately, that's a family known for being bold. Let me see if I can answer your question." He made a brief phone call. "They're already thinking about it."

"You've been to Mars. This should be a walk in the park."

"Maybe so but you still haven't said why JPL is interested."

"I didn't say JPL was interested. I'm interested. Who do I talk to about joining the team?"

It was his turn to smile. "Well, Margot, how do you feel about Texas?"

Margot had never been to Brownsville, and her first impression was if she never saw it again, that would be fine. However, it was the closest public airport to SpaceX's launch facility at Bolsa Chica Beach. She was traveling on her own dime and using vacation time from JPL. She thought it would be prudent to rent a Tesla, but Avis had none available. Instead, she drove the ten miles out of town in something non-descript from Japan or Korea that smelled bad.

The guard was expecting her. He directed her to the office behind the hangar and beside the weld shop. The receptionist showed her to the personnel director. She dropped a business card on her keyboard and introduced herself. The nameplate on the desk said, Donna Lyons.

"I'm happy to meet you, Ms. Medina, but tell me again why we need an astrophysicist on this mission."

Margot grinned. "Everybody needs an astrophysicist."

The woman rolled her eyes and returned the grin. "Have a seat. So, are you applying for employment with SpaceX, or is this more of a hobby with you?"

"Well, I wouldn't call it a hobby. I intend to maintain my employment with JPL. I've spoken with my supervisor who is on board with me participating in this mission."

"You do know astronaut training process takes two years."

"Yeah, I'm okay with that."

"You will be cutting it close. This mission lifts off in twenty-two months."

"Then the sooner I get started the better."

"I can't just approve you. We have a questionnaire you'll have to complete. We're willing to fast-track you, but we can't cut corners." Lyons took a tablet from the bookcase behind her. "The questionnaire is on here. You can use the lunchroom. It should be quiet this time of day. Come see me when you're finished."

Margot took the tablet and read the display. "Is it timed?"

"No, it's not a test. It asks about your health history and some general questions about your aptitude to complete the training process. Ask the receptionist to direct you to the lunchroom."

It took an hour to complete the questions. Margot took the tablet back to Donna Lyons. "Here you go. When do I find out if I passed?"

"Oh, you passed. The tablet sent me a text. How soon can you get to Houston?"

"If I can get a flight, I can be there tonight."

"Good. Report to the Johnson Training Center first thing in the morning. The necessary paperwork will be waiting for you. Good luck." She stood to shake hands.

From the bar in the Brownsville airport, she called her supervisor. "I got accepted. I'm going straight to Houston."

"How long will you be gone?" he asked.

"The whole two years plus the mission time."

"Crap."

"Are you changing your mind?"

She heard a deep sigh. "No, I'll keep you on payroll. Nobody will notice one absent astrophysicist."

"Technically, I'll still be working for NASA."

"Yeah, I know. It all comes out of the same pocket. Well, have fun. Check-in once in a while."

"Okay. I'll bring you a souvenir from the rogue planet."

"Can't wait. Ciao."

NASA's Johnson Space Center sprawled for mostly empty miles. The guard at the gate she chose gave her a map with the intake center highlighted. She still got lost. Finally, a man driving an electric cart led her to the right building. The woman at the reception desk wore a blue NASA uniform. She was a little on the chunky side and did not look like astronaut material. She did, however, have Margot's paperwork.

"Your first stop, after you sign in, is the tailor shop, so we can take measurements for your space suit. When you're finished there, come back and we'll assign you a docent to show you the ropes."

Margot dutifully signed after half a dozen Xs and she pinned a badge to her blouse, then she followed a blue line on the floor to the tailor shop. She expected to be measured with a tape. Nope. Too low-tech. She was scanned, so it didn't take long. "How long does it take to make my spacesuit?" she asked.

The friendly young female technician said, "Only a few days. You'll need it before you do much of anything in the training program. You will also get some coveralls and a few of those spiffy blue jumpsuits."

The docent was a thirtyish woman with an engaging smile and the gift of gab. She gave Margot a binder. "This is your schedule for the whole training program. Today I'm going to familiarize you with the campus. Tomorrow and the next day you'll have classwork. When you get your kit, then you can start doing some real training. Each morning starts with fitness training. Ready? Follow me."

"What do I call you?" Margot asked.

She held her badge while grinning. It said, 'Marge.'

Marge drove her in a golf cart to all the pertinent buildings, showed her the tram stops, and her quarters. They broke for lunch, then she got to meet her crewmates. Jason Martin looked like an ad for the Marine Corp. He looked Margot over and said, "You the new chick from JPL?"

Xavier Moreno was, well *moreno*. He said, *"¿Qué tal, chiquita?"*

Carter Ross had red hair, fair skin, and blue eyes.

She looked her crewmates over, ran her tongue around her teeth, and said, "If toxic masculinity had three faces…"

Carter Ross' smile radiated. "This mission just got better looking."

Margot had outgrown blushing. She returned his smile, shook his hand, and said, "Thank you. You're not so bad yourself. You two, we'll wait and see."

CHAPTER 3

The classwork was boring and tedious. There was only one other would-be astronaut in her class, a young Japanese guy whose English was iffy. When she got her spacesuit, things got livelier. She was then able to train with her crewmates in the gigantic Neutral Buoyancy pool, on the Air-Bearing floor where they practiced handling large objects in micro-gravity. Then there was the Vomit Comet where they experienced genuine weightlessness for a few seconds as the big airplane performed aerobatics. The centrifuge machine put Margot in mind of Space Mountain at Disneyland. It also made her sick.

"Don't feel bad," Jason told her. "We all puked on that thing."

"Thanks. Nothing I like better than throwing up into own hair."

Carter Ross said, "It brings out the blond highlights."

She was most fond of Carter and gently encouraged his attention when they were alone. Naturally, fraternization was frowned upon by the brass.

Weeks turned into months. Images of their object arrived periodically from the Hubble telescope. The dot of light grew more defined, but it was still too far away to see any detail on the surface.

They were studying Hubble's images late one afternoon on a wide-screen monitor in the bar when Xavier asked, "What if it's a space ark?"

"Wouldn't that be cool?" Margot said.

Carter replied, "Only if they like uninvited guests."

She grinned mischievously. "Carter, we'll let you make first contact. I'm sure you could charm your way into their good graces."

"So, I get the 'take me to your leader' moment?"

"Absolutely," Jason said, "we unanimously voted you the sacrificial lamb."

Xavier said, "We also voted that it's your turn to buy."

"How come I never get to vote?"

"Because of your felony record," Xavier laughed.

"What did I do?"

"We don't know, but we're sure you did something."

That broke the group up, and Margot signaled for another round.

"Seriously," Xavier said, "did you all read Arthur Clarke's *Rendezvous with Rama?*"

The two men nodded. Margot said, "No, what's it about?"

"Space ark. This big cylinder enters the solar system, but all it's got inside it are weird animals. The only alien is a mummy."

Her eyes widened. "Now, I remember. When that asteroid thing that they gave an Hawaiian name flew by people were talking about Rama."

"That's right, but it turned out to be a rock," Carter said.

"We should have sent a mission to it. How do we know it wasn't a hollow rock?" Margot asked.

Jason raised his beer. "At least we're not going to make the same mistake twice."

"We can hope," Carter said. "Have you heard the FAA is trying to stop launches from Bolsa Chica?"

Margo said, "They can't do that."

"Hell," Jason said, "we can pack up and go to Florida to launch if we have to."

"Just so it doesn't delay us past our launch window." Margot took a sip of the gin and tonic she had developed a taste for.

Xavier knocked back his tequila, licked the salt off his hand, and bit a lime wedge, then he belched. "Let's get back to what if it's artificial and occupied."

"Oh, gross," Margot said of the belch. "That's decided. We let Carter handle it."

"What if they shoot first?"

"Then it won't matter." She smiled briefly.

"I still think we need some kind of defensive weapon. You guys gonna have another round?"

Jason laughed and choked on his beer. "What are we gonna shoot it with? The thing's ten thousand miles in diameter."

"Go ahead and have another tequila, Xavier," Margot said, "then you'll be able to whip any alien's ass."

Carter said, "Anybody hungry? Wanna share some ribs?"

"Sure," Xavier said, "since it's your night to buy."

He glared at him before waving for the waitress. "Sweetheart, bring us a couple orders of ribs, please and plenty of napkins. And we'll have another round except for this Mexican asshole. He's cut off."

She cocked her head with a hand on her hip. "How you gonna cut him off if you don't know where he's getting it? Same all around?"

The night went downhill from there.

The following morning, the crew flew to Bolsa Chica by helicopter to inspect their Starship.

"It's huge," Margot cried when she saw the hundred-and-sixty-foot-tall spacecraft.

"And it's not even on its booster," Jason added.

"Well, you didn't want to be crowded, did you?" Carter said.

21

Margot lowered her voice. "I like to feel cozy." That earned her a sly look.

Before they were allowed to inspect it, they had to decontaminate and don paper clean-suits. Inside was only half the length of the thing. The lower half was fuel tanks and six Raptor engines. There was a flight deck, galley, and sleeping quarters. There was also a cargo hold that contained a four-passenger rover.

"All the comforts of home," Margot said.

"It needs a bar," Carter added.

A SpaceX flight engineer gave them operation manuals—they were an inch thick—then he lectured on the controls and instruments for two solid hours. He finished with, "Any questions?"

Xavier asked, "What's for lunch?"

The engineer ignored him. "We are shipping a simulator to Houston. The rest of your training will be in that."

Jason was a colonel in the Air Force, which designated him crew captain. It was not in his nature to flaunt his rank. He was in the pilot's seat the first time they attempted a simulated landing. They crashed.

Carter said, "That went well."

Eventually, each of them successfully landed the Starship. It was not yet known if the planet had an atmosphere, so it was necessary to practice landing with and without the use of the stabilizer wings. The ship had four stubby wings—two fore, two aft. They were, of course, no use in a vacuum.

Jason smiled when Margot aced her atmospheric landing. "Girl, you're the only one of us who never crashed. I think we'll let you drive."

"That's because you cowboys drive on testosterone."

"Damn right," Carter said.

"I still think we need some nukes," Xavier added.

"What happened to 'we come in peace'?" Margot asked.

"We don't have to use them if the natives are friendly."

Jason held up his hands. "Who's for calling it a day and knocking a few back while we check out the latest Hubble images?"

It was a silly question.

The images were updated daily. It was now a well-defined disk and not just a point of light. Margot put on her astrophysicist hat. She left the table, went to the bar, and leaned toward the monitor.

"See that star right by the edge of the disk? If it had an atmosphere, that star would look fuzzy, but it's perfectly sharp," she said when she returned to the table.

Xavier had switched to Margaritas. "I never said they were living on the surface. Of course, they're inside."

Jason shook his head. "If the inside of that thing was warm enough for aliens, don't you think we would detect some infrared radiation?"

"It's well insulated."

Margot almost spit her drink. "Xavier, you should write science fiction stories."

"Maybe I will."

Carter had been strangely quiet. "How disappointed are we going to be if it turns out to be just a big, dead rock?"

"We'd best be prepared for that," Jason said.

"Don't be a party pooper," Margot told him.

"What are you expecting?"

"An interesting big, dead rock." That earned her a laugh.

CHAPTER 4

Margot and Carter left the bar. The other two were going to stay to watch a basketball game. It was a balmy night as they sat together at a newly installed tram stop. Margot said, "Carter, are you ever going to make a move on me?"

He looked like he'd seen a ghost. "Are you trying to tell me something?"

"I know you're not gay, and I know you're not shy."

"I didn't think you were interested in me."

"Up until now, I didn't think you were dumb. For Chrissake, kiss me."

He started to put an arm around her. The tram came.

Margot said, "Shit."

The tram stopped by her barracks. She stood and grabbed Carter's upper arm. "This is your stop too."

"Yes, ma'am."

There was nobody in the hall, and she managed to get him into her room without anyone seeing them—not that she cared or thought anyone else would.

Carter turned her by the arm and completed that aborted kiss. Margot led him to her bed and took the initiative. When they were finished, she said, "Don't wake me when you go out."

Carter was late for fitness training the following morning. Margot sidled close to him and whispered, "Was I that hard on you?"

"It was one of those seeing the face of God moments."

Before she could form a witty reply, their fitness coach said, "Folks, I need your attention." When the gym fell quiet, he continued, "NASA has decided to pull funding for your training. This will be your last week."

"Why?" Margot asked.

"Just bureaucratic bullshit. Congress would rather spend money on missiles for Poland and welfare for illegals than on spaceflight."

Jason said, "I don't get it. SpaceX is funding this mission."

"Yeah, it's only the training NASA is pulling the plug on."

"Jesus, we were almost done," Carter moaned.

"There's no reason you can't wrap it up at Bolsa Chica. Just get the simulator shipped back there."

Margot said, "The damn government is going to screw around and make us miss our launch window."

"That's what they do best," the coach said. "Now, back on the treadmill. You're still mine until the end of the week."

SpaceX rented them a house off-site. It was in Bolsa Chica Village a mile or so from the base. It had four bedrooms, but Margot and Carter came out of the closet and shared one. Instead of treadmills, the team jogged on the beach in the morning. After breakfast, it was back in the simulator until it was time to try a mock launch in the real Starship. It now sat atop the gleaming stainless steel booster, which made it the tallest spacecraft ever built.

It was anticlimactic, because the launch was handled by computers. All the crew had to do was report on the readiness of the various systems. They pretended to take off and accelerate until the ejection of the booster. It went off without a hitch. When it was over, the flight controller said, "Okay, kids, in three days, it's for real."

SpaceX issued a press release to announce the launch. The FAA promptly served them a cease-and-desist order. The crew heard the explosion from the executive office all the way back in their house in the village. The army of lawyers that descended on the Fifth Circuit Court in Tyler, Texas, had to be billing SpaceX an aggregate of twenty grand per hour.

Back at Bolsa Chica, Margot was blistering the ears of her crewmates with her diatribe against the government.

When she paused to take a breath, Carter said with a huge grin, "Tell us how you really feel about it."

Xavier said, *"Tranquila, chica. Me pones sordo."*

Jason made a call to the flight controller. He stabbed the end icon. "They started fueling. They can't stop."

"So, what are the options?"

"I told you we needed nukes," Xavier said and reached for the tequila bottle.

Margot said, "Pour one for me."

"If we can't get an injunction," Jason said, "we launch and pay a fine. I can't imagine the Feds trying to stop us by force."

The suspense made for a long forty-eight hours.

Newsmax covered the story by interviewing flight controller Avery. "This is nothing but political BS. The FAA controls commercial aircraft. All they have to do is route traffic around us the same way they do at Canaveral. That Starship is launching tomorrow. Fuck 'em if they can't take a joke." Newsmax bleeped him.

Before sunrise, a van came for the crew. The spaceport looked like a military base. Armed security waited in Humvees outside the perimeter fence. The driver said, "We're not expecting law enforcement, but old man Avery says he's prepared for a standoff."

Inside the compound, they ate steak and eggs, donned their spacesuits, and rode the elevator to the top of the gantry four hundred feet above the launch pad. They settled into their respective recliners and were double-checked by the gantry technicians who gave them thumbs up as they sealed the hatch on their way out of the Starship. Then they waited. Every ten minutes, they were advised of the countdown. They had fifty minutes remaining.

At T-minus thirty-five, there was a hold. They heard Avery's voice, "People, we have an issue. There are military aircraft in the flight path."

Margot said, "Shit. Do they think they're going to shoot us down?"

"Never underestimate the Feds' ability to fuck things up."

Jason keyed his mic. "Are we in contact with these aircraft?"

"Negative. We're communicating with our legal team. Will advise."

A dreary hour crawled past.

"Hey, Carter," Margot said, "you wanna slip back to the sleeping quarters?"

"Cool your jets, Medina," Jason said flatly.

"Gotta do something to pass the time."

Xavier said, "I can't believe we're sitting on a few tons of liquid methane waiting for a lawyer."

"We're going to be here a while," Jason said, "FAA brass and federal judges are still in bed."

"Has anybody ever explained why the FAA has a hard-on for us?" Margot asked.

Jason replied, "I've never heard what their problem is, but the battle goes back to when this place was built—"

"T-minus thirty and counting." The timekeeper startled them.

Jason said, "What happened?"

Avery's voice came over the intercom. "The Fifth Circuit issued a restraining order. The sky is empty once more." They could hear cheering in the control room.

Carter said, "Say hallelujah."

"You missed your chance, Carter," Margot said. "Now, we're stuck here for the next thirty minutes."

"I'm looking forward to weightlessness."

"Oh, yeah?"

The minutes ticked past. In the last sixty seconds, pulse rates rose. All systems had been confirmed. No one spoke but the timekeeper. On 'ignition' the methane ignited, the Starship shuddered, then there was liftoff. Margot imagined crowds on the beach shading their eyes as the black spaceship atop the shining booster rose on the huge tail of flame. For a moment, she felt the sting of tears. The voice of the flight controller droned, but the roar of the engines drowned what he was saying. Their lives were completely out of their control. They were in the hands of the precision of technology and manufacturing and were riding the most innovative machine ever built.

CHAPTER 5

The rogue planet had been christened Odysseus. The Starship had also been given a name. It was the Argo. Jason wanted to call his crewmates the Argonauts. They objected on the grounds that his head was already too big. The mission to rendezvous with Odysseus would take two months—sixty-two days and eight hours to be exact. They would orbit until a safe landing zone was found. Once the Argo was on the ground, the team had fourteen days to explore and collect samples. There was little for the crew to do while in flight. Jason and Xavier amused themselves by making fun of the inordinate amount of time Carter and Margot spent in private. Margot gave as good as she got. Carter kept his mouth shut and counted his blessings.

The galley was well stocked and functional, so meals were a way to pass the time. Margot could cook and so could Xavier. They competed to see who could prepare the most elaborate dinners. The coolest gadget was a centrifuge microwave.

Telemetry delivered new images from the Hubble Space Telescope. Good as they were, surface detail remained invisible. Conversation rarely strayed far from what they were going to find.

"We're probably going to find evidence of a major impact," Margot told the men.

"That makes sense," Carter said. "Something had to knock it loose from its star."

"Models still show it not affecting Earth's orbit, but I can't shake the idea that it's getting pretty close," Xavier fretted.

"To be honest," Margot said, "I can't either. It has a lot of gravitational pull."

News from home continued dire—food shortages, racial unrest, and inflation. The Russians still had a blockade around Warsaw, and NATO refused to intervene in spite of Article 5's promise of support.

Xavier asked, "What do you all think will happen back home when we tell them Odysseus is a space ark?"

"People will go more nuts than they already are," Margot said.

"Give it a rest," Carter said. "You've been reading too many sci-fi stories."

"You'll see. Only five days now."

Jason had been staring at a monitor with the image of Odysseus in real-time. He roused himself from being transfixed. "Medina, do you want to make the landing? You have the best record in the simulator."

"So you can beat up on me if I crash us?"

"If you crash us, we'll be dead."

"Well, in that case, fine."

Jason smiled. "I'll be backup in case you're having PMS or something. Carter, you read the altimeter. Xavier, you shoot at the aliens."

On day sixty-two at two PM Texas time, Jason maneuvered the Argo into orbit at one hundred and fifty miles above the surface. The daylight side could have been Mars. There were some features visible, large craters and mountains—no ice, no clouds, certainly no vegetation.

"Looks pretty barren," Jason said.

"Not going to be hard to pick a landing spot," Margot said looking at her monitor.

After an orbit, the captain said, "It all looks the same to me. Let's take it down. Medina, you have the helm."

"You didn't ask me about PMS."

"I'm feeling fatalistic. Go for it. Equator is as good as any place."

Margot slowed the Argo and oriented it for vertical descent. In truth, the computer did most of the work. She monitored their descent and made sure the landing struts deployed. For seconds they hovered just feet off the ground, then settled gently.

Carter said, "Perfect. Sensors say we're on hard ground and vertical within two degrees."

Jason keyed his mic. "Bolsa Chica, Argo has met Odysseus."

"Systems report," Jason said.

33

Xavier replied, "All good here."

"Same," said Carter.

"Let's go see this sucker." Margot was already out of her seat.

After donning spacesuits, it took an hour or so to get the dune buggy out of the cargo hold. There were also some experiments they had to perform— taking soil samples, three-sixty-degree panoramic video, and ground-penetrating radar.

Margot finished transmitting the video. "All right. Enough stalling. Let's go for a ride."

Jason asked her, "You want to drive?"

"No, go ahead. I want to sightsee."

The sun appeared half the size as it did from Earth. The landscape was rocky and dusty brown with reddish traces on the horizon, which appeared exactly as far away as home. There were mountains to the north. Jason headed for them.

"Keep your eyes out for the entrance to the interior," Xavier said.

"Don't forget, Carter goes in first," Jason reminded.

Margot asked, "How are we going to know what the code is for the portal's keypad?"

"We'll just knock," Xavier said.

On the plain, there was nothing of interest. It took less than an hour to reach the hills. Jason maneuvered through passes and approached the summit. "Who wants to bet a buck on what's on the other side?"

Xavier said, "The portal."

Carter said, "A theme park."

Margot said, "More rocks."

After a moment, Jason said, "I bet bigger rocks." He floored the drive pedal and shot over the gravelly summit. "Oh, my God."

CHAPTER 6

Jason whispered, "Holy shit."

"Stop," Margot shouted. "Let me send Bolsa Chica a video." She stood in the passenger seat and recorded a video of the scene below them. "What if SpaceX hadn't funded this mission?"

"We should have gone to that other rock we were talking about," Xavier said.

"What'd they call that thing?" Jason asked.

"Something like Emu-amua. This proves it was a space ark."

Carter groaned.

"Yeah, well we give the world downtown Odysseus." Margot transmitted her video. "So, quit fucking around. Get us down there."

From the distance, the buildings looked human-sized but grew massively on close inspection. They entered the city on a smoothly paved street. Xavier studied the fronts of the buildings. "These guys must have been ten feet tall."

"Yeah, maybe it's time to send Carter ahead of us," Margot joked.

Jason said, "Things are remarkably well preserved."

"Let's go inside one of them," Margot said.

Xavier said, "We should have brought guns."

Carter shook his head. "If there's anybody still living on this rock, they've been holding their breath for a hell of a long time."

Jason stopped the rover by an open doorway. "You suppose I'll get a ticket for parking here?"

Margot was already out of the vehicle and inspecting the opening. "There was never a door here."

"I guess they were the trusting type." Carter stepped beside her and ran his gloved hand over the featureless doorframe. "No hinges, no latch, no jamb."

"What do you suppose these walls are made of?" Margot tapped it with the corner of her video transmitter.

Jason touched it as well. "We have to get a sample. Whatever it is, it's seamless—like it was cast in place."

"That's not so strange," Xavier said. "We cast concrete."

The group moved inside. "The ceiling must be twenty feet high," Margot said.

"This room is the size of a gymnasium, but there's nothing in it." Carter turned around. "Anybody bring a flashlight?"

There was a collective 'no.'

Margot went to the far wall, touched it, and followed the walls back to the doorway. "A big, empty room. Let's go in another building. There must be some artifacts somewhere."

They crossed the street, which would have accommodated four Earthly lanes of traffic. The building they entered was again large and empty.

Stepping back into the street, Carter said, "There's no signage."

"This is a very strange place," Margot said. "Let's split up so we can cover more ground."

"Only two and two," Jason said, "in case of accidents."

"Or aliens," Xavier added. Carter shoved him.

Jason gestured to Carter and Margot. "I don't want to find you two shacked up somewhere. Take the other side of the street. The *hombre* and I will take this side."

The next building Margot and Carter entered had a back room. It had windows with no sign of having been glazed. There was nothing in either room. Margot looked at the high ceiling. "No fixtures, no furniture—these guys were minimalists."

"And nothing is in ruins. How many millennia has this place been abandoned?"

"Well, it helps that there's no vegetation."

"Yeah, but...it's hardly even dusty." He bent down and stroked the floor.

"Come on. Let's keep moving. There has to be something interesting somewhere—some clue as to what they were like."

"Apparently, they were big and slept on the floor."

She scowled at him, though she knew he couldn't see it through her faceplate. "Any culture that could build these buildings had to have stuff."

They continued searching finding little variation in the buildings until they both heard Jason's voice. "Hey, you two, double-time it back to the rover. Xavier's got just enough oh-two to make it back to the ship."

Margot keyed her mic. "Crap. Tell him to hold his breath."

The diminutive sun in the black sky had almost reached the horizon when they reached the airlock. Back on the flight deck and in coveralls once more, they made a report to Bolsa Chica. It took seven minutes to get a reply.

"You kids were stars before. Now, you're superstars. The media is going crazy over your videos. Get some rest, then do some more exploring. Good luck and play nice with the aliens."

Xavier said, "See. Even they know they're out there somewhere."

"I hate to rain on your space ark parade," Jason said, "but ground-penetrating radar did not indicate a hollow core."

"It's probably only half hollow."

"Okay, guys," Margot began, "tomorrow do we keep exploring the same place, or do we go looking for another city?"

Carter said, "Let's look for another one. Maybe there's a reason why that one is empty. Maybe it was just under construction."

Margot rubbed her chin. "Interesting thought. I agree. We don't want to have to leave here in thirteen days without knowing something about this culture."

Jason said, "Check. Tomorrow remember to take lights, and we'll take the spare oxygen bottles."

"I should have sneaked my 9mm on board," Xavier grumbled.

"Who's up for cheeseburgers?" Margot asked.

The sun was well up when Jason steered the rover in a new direction. It only took a few minutes to find a highway. They followed it and soon discerned the profile of buildings on the horizon. Again, the city streets were free of debris. The doorways gaped emptily.

"Let's keep driving so we know the size of this place," Margot said while recording video.

Jason turned from the street that led them to the ruins. "These places seem to be laid out in grids."

"I wonder if we could get on the roof of a building," Carter said. "They are all one story."

"We haven't seen anything that looks like a stairway," Xavier replied.

Margot quit shooting videos. "Let's recap what we see—empty buildings with no sign of what they're made of, no trace of writing, no furniture, or artifacts of any kind. Look close at the streets. There is no infrastructure like sewers or traffic control. There are no doors or glass in the windows."

Carter asked, "What does that tell us about them?"

"Not a damn thing."

"Well," Xavier said, "they were probably a lot bigger than us."

Margot said, "What I want to know is where are the bodies?"

CHAPTER 7

Their explorations were limited by their air supply and the rover's batteries which only recharged when the sun was in the black sky. In ten days, they had found and explored four cities that varied very little. They also found a great basin that surely must have been a sea. The sea yielded some fossils of remarkably Earthlike shellfish.

Over linguini with clam sauce, Margot said, "Even if they had time to evacuate—and take every stitch of their belongings with them—they must have had cemeteries."

"They also must have had spaceports." Jason twirled some pasta on his fork.

"Yeah, we should have looked for that from orbit."

"I don't know," Carter said. "You can't tell what Canaveral is from orbit. The only manmade object you can see from space is the Great Wall of China."

"Aren't we an encyclopedia today?" she chided.

"I just don't want you beating yourself up because we only took one orbit."

"Don't worry about that. I can always forgive myself."

Jason looked up from his linguini. "Listen up. Incoming message from home."

The speaker in the galley crackled. "Attention, Argonauts, this is mission control. We have some new information for you. Odysseus is apparently more massive than we thought. The sun is deflecting its trajectory into a tighter curve than anticipated. This means it is following the orbit of Earth more closely than we first predicted, therefore, you could stay another fourteen days, translocate, and still have enough fuel to reach Earth orbit. We could then send a Dragon Cargo module to rendezvous and refuel you. Your food supply should be adequate unless you've been pigging out. Please advise your decision."

The four looked from one another with mixed expressions.

Margot broke the ice. "I say we go for it."

Carter said, "What could go wrong?"

"I'm for it," Xavier said. "We need to find the portal."

Jason shrugged his shoulders. "No way I'm going to be a pussy about it, but let's do a couple low polar orbits and look for someplace interesting."

"Works for me," Margot said. "Let Bolsa Chica know."

Jason said to his mic, "Roger mission control, will translocate after minimum two polar orbits soon as the dishes are done."

The seven minutes it took the reply to arrive seemed like eternity. "Check. Polar orbit is a good idea but no lower than a hundred twenty miles and no more than three or you could burn too much fuel."

"Got it. Will advise safe landing."

Seven minutes later, Avery's sarcastic voice said, "Do not advise unsafe landing. Out."

They hurried through the rest of the meal and assumed their positions. Jason called for the prelaunch system checks, then initiated the launch sequences. Slowly, the Starship rose from the surface of Odysseus, and the gees increased. Each crewmember continued to monitor their assigned systems and announced the results. Finally, the ship achieved orbital altitude, and the computer shut down the Raptor engines.

Margot increased magnification on her monitor to its max. "You still can't see anything."

"Keep your eyes peeled for the portal," Xavier reminded.

"Yeah, right."

Jason said, "Carter, monitor our distance from the surface. It won't do us any good to land at the bottom of a seabed."

"Check."

After thirty minutes, Margot said, "That area to the left is colored a little different. How about we tilt our next orbit to fly over it?"

"Will do," Jason replied.

"Oh, wait." Margot's voice rose. "Right there—those shadows don't look natural."

Carter said, "You're imagining things."

"I'll bet you a buck those are buildings."

"Okay," Jason said, "mark the spot."

"I think she's right," Xavier agreed. "It's a big area, and it looks different than the surrounding terrain."

"Keep watching," Jason said. "We're going to take another lap."

Margot thought she spotted another city in the southern hemisphere.

An hour later, as they emerged from the dark side, Jason asked, "Okay, fun seekers, which one do we land beside?"

Margot said, "I vote for the one in the northern hemisphere. I think it looked bigger."

"Carter, was it above sea level?" Jason asked.

"Yep."

"All right. Take us down, Medina. You're the pro at smooth landings."

She turned the ship and pulsed the rockets, achieved vertical status, and began the descent. The stabilizers deployed, she hovered momentarily, then gently set it down.

Carter hooted. "You're getting better. We're half a degree off vertical."

She mimed polishing her nails on her jumpsuit.

"Okay, you know the drill. Moreno and I will get the rover out. You two do the experiments," Jason said.

An hour later, they were riding toward what they hoped was another city.

Margot began taking video as soon as buildings were recognizable. "Holy shit. What do you make of this?"

Carter was sitting beside her. "It looks like a damn city. Now, what do we make of those we saw before?"

"Maybe they were under construction."

"We never saw anything that looked unfinished—no building materials laying around, no tools."

Xavier said, "There'll be a portal to the interior in this one."

"Maybe there will be bodies in this one," Jason said twisting in the driver's seat.

The city began abruptly. The buildings were multi-storied with doors and glazing in the windows. They were extremely varied. Most were rectangular, but many were cylindrical. Some were abstract stacks of boxes. Streets meandered randomly and were dotted with what were apparently light sources—some on poles, some hanging from walls. There were sidewalks and things that appeared to be ornamental, but there was virtually no open space.

"Okay, kids," Jason said, "let's do some exploring, but we stay together. We could get lost in this place."

The building they entered—through a conventional enough swinging door—had fixtures and what they took to be furniture.

Margot stood in front of one example. "This is a chair. Whatever sat it in had bendable legs and was quite a bit taller than us."

"It has no armrests," Carter noted.

"Not all human chairs have armrests."

"Just saying."

"I wonder how we get upstairs," Xavier said.

Jason grinned at him. "I thought you were only interested in the portal to the underworld."

"I wonder about that too."

"That's how you get upstairs," Carter said pointing to a ramp at the far end of the spacious room.

The ceiling was perhaps twelve feet high. The ramp required two flights to reach the second floor.

"What does a ramp say about their locomotion?" Margot mused.

Carter replied, "There may be steps in other places. They probably have elevators too."

"Right," she quipped, "and armrests."

The second floor was divided into rooms—some had doors, some didn't. One chamber had the remains of what was clearly a bed.

The mattress was a sort of gel. It was chest high to Margot. "They must have been over eight feet tall, and that being the case, unless they were really skinny, this is a single bed."

Carter gave her a meaningful look. "You make something of that?"

"Not yet, but I prefer my aliens to be libidinous."

"How do you know they didn't divide like amoebas?"

"Eew, that wouldn't be any fun at all."

"You've got a one-track mind but don't ever change."

"All right, you two, let's get serious," Jason interrupted. "Medina, you getting this on video?"

"Yes, chief."

"Is there a ramp to the third floor," he asked.

"Nope," Xavier replied. "I've looked in every door. You can't get there from here."

"But this building must have ten stories," Margot said.

"Maybe there's a ramp well," Carter said.

"A what?"

"You know, like a stairwell but a ramp well."

"You mean that has access from outside?" she asked.

"There's got to be some way to get up there."

Jason took charge. "Let's go outside and walk around the place."

They didn't find any other entrance.

"How the hell did they get up there?" Margot wondered.

"Levitation," Xavier suggested.

"Nothing about this place will surprise me," Jason said.

Margot shook her head inside her helmet. "I still want to know where are the damn bodies?"

CHAPTER 8

Bolsa Chica gushed over the day's videos. In the communication that evening, Avery told them, "We're assembling a team of experts—anthropologists, biologists, architects, you name it. They're going to try to put together a theory of what those beings were like. Get us some more good stuff tomorrow."

Over dinner, Margot recapped the day's assumptions. "We know they were bigger than us, they had bendable legs, they most likely slept—"

"Alone," Carter interrupted.

She glared at him. "And they had some kind of technology for getting into upstairs apartments without steps or elevators."

"What I want to know is why the big difference in the two types of architecture?" Jason pondered.

Margot replied without hesitating, "Maybe there were two species."

"But neither of them left any skeletons?" Carter said. "That's weird."

"That's more than weird. Okay, big guy, what are we going to do tomorrow?"

Jason answered her, "We're going to investigate more buildings. What else? Sooner or later we're going to find something that identifies these guys."

Xavier broke his silence. "There has to be some artwork or family portraits somewhere."

"Another strange thing is the lack of suburbs," Carter added. "There are no single-family units."

"And what about vehicles?" Xavier continued. "They had roads. Something had to drive on them."

Margot scratched her chin. "That two-story unit we were in had nothing like a kitchen—no utensils, no groceries, no knick-knacks."

"And no bathroom," Carter said.

"Eew, that's gross," Xavier grimaced.

Margot rose and put her plate in the dishwasher. "I'm going to bed." She turned to Carter. "Alone."

The building they chose to explore the following morning was a cylindrical tower. There was no door at the entry. It opened into a foyer that contained what could only be a reception desk. In the center of the space rose another cylinder with a ramp spiraling its periphery.

"All right, kids," Jason said, "let's see if we can get above the second floor in this one."

The ramp did indeed extend all the way to the top floor at which, through a simple door with hinges, they emerged onto the roof.

"Cool," Margot said standing on her toes to see over the chin-high parapet, "great view."

"Yeah," Carter agreed, "the place is huge."

"See anything that looks like a spaceport?" Jason asked.

"It wouldn't be in the city, would it?"

"Who knows? I can't explain anything about this place."

"Something just occurred to me," Margot said, "there's no plumbing so no water. What kind of creature can live without water?"

Jason gestured to follow. "Taking in the view isn't answering any questions. Let's go inside."

The apartment on the top floor had a bedchamber with a single bed, a chair with armrests, and a piece of furniture like a dresser. Instead of drawers, doors opened to several compartments. All were empty.

"So," Carter said looking at the chair, "we've confirmed arms and legs, but we still don't know how many of each."

"Let's try to investigate every room in this building," Margot suggested. "I'm thinking maybe there is a communal kitchen and bath."

A floor at the vertical center of the tower had a communal feel about it. There was only one big, circular space with too many chairs to count. Margot took video, but of course, the room was dark and there was no way she could capture the whole space in one image. The light on her camera could only illuminate so much. "Okay, let's say they came here to eat, where is the prep area?"

"Where is the toilet?" Carter asked.

"Carter," Margot said, "get your head out of the toilet."

"Maybe it's on the floor below us," Xavier said.

It wasn't. The rest of the floors were like those above—a sleeping chamber and sitting areas.

When they finished looking into the rest of the floors, it was time to return to the ship. On the trip back, Jason said, "Tomorrow I propose we just drive around. Maybe we'll find something that makes sense."

The message from mission control that night was, "Curiouser and curiouser."

The vastness of the city amazed the explorers. Margot said, "It's as big as greater Los Angeles."

"A lot nicer though," Carter added.

"Yeah," Xavier said, "where's the *barrios?*"

Nothing seemed to change—high-rise buildings of various designs, a maze of streets, and no open spaces. Well over an hour into the day's tour, Jason took his foot off the accelerator. "Whoa, boys and girls, this is different." Before them stretched an enormous empty space. It was paved, and it easily encompassed ten miles square.

"I think we found the spaceport," Margot ventured.

"Yeah," Jason said pointing, "and look at the size of that building to the left." He began driving toward it. "It's a hangar. Look at those doors." There were large windows over what were clearly hangar doors. Above the row of glass, the roof was domed. Jason circumnavigated the building. Looking at the odometer, he said, "The place is over two miles long by a mile deep. There's an open door. Should we go in it?"

Margot shook her head behind her visor. "Don't be a silly ass. Of course, we're going in."

Inside, the headlights and spotlight revealed a mostly empty space. Massive shapes in the distance materialized into huge pieces of machinery. A pyramid roll the length of a football field was easily identified. Great flat-topped trucks that could carry their starship parked against the walls.

Xavier said pointing at the rolling machine, "With that big sucker, they could roll the fuselage of our starship in one piece. This is their space ark factory."

Carter looked above the doors. "Where are the windows?"

"There's a floor above all this," Margot said. "We need to find the ramp."

Jason drove beneath a behemoth bridge-style gantry with electrodes at the end of articulated arms. "Ask and ye shall receive." He stopped at the foot of a spiral ramp. "Shall we?"

After a wearying climb, they emerged into a mammoth room full of identical chairs. They crossed it to the bank of windows and looked into the black void. "Dammit," Margot said, "I wish we could turn on the lights."

Carter shined his flashlight around the room full of alien chairs. "Yeah, that would be nice. My guess is this was their engineering department."

"Engineering without desks?" she asked.

"I doubt if they used pencils and paper."

Xavier had wandered to the far end of the room. "Hey," he shouted, "come see this."

The trio joined him at the archway into the adjoining chamber.

"Holy shit," Margot whispered.

Crystals—bank after bank of multi-colored crystals extended as far as their flashlight beams projected.

Jason gasped, "What do you make of it?"

The astrophysicist answered, "My guess is it's a computer."

All three men turned toward her. Carter asked, "What the—"

"We use crystals in electronics. You could use different frequencies to represent numbers, or simply one frequency equals zero while another equals one if you want to remain binary. You surely don't think these are here because they're pretty."

Jason said, "If you say so."

"Then this must be what runs the machines that built the space arks," Xavier said.

Carter shook his head inside his helmet. "You and your space arks."

Margot walked toward a crystal a little taller than her. "This is the closest thing to an artifact we've found." She ran her hand down the smooth side. "Hey, it's vibrating."

Jason quickly joined her. "How can that be if there's no power?"

"Okay, now, that one is beyond me," she admitted.

Xavier touched another crystal. "Be damned. Let's figure out how to fire it up and build our own space ark."

Carter groaned.

"How much time have we got left?" she asked Jason.

He looked at his chronometer. "Not a lot but let's look around. Maybe we can find the control panel."

Their search found nothing resembling a control panel.

"Dammit," Margot swore, "I wish we could find their version of a laptop to take home with us. I'm beginning to think they operated their stuff telepathically."

"That's a pretty good theory," Jason said. "But now, kids, we've got to get back."

CHAPTER 9

What are we going to do tomorrow, fearless leader?" Margot asked Jason during dinner.

"I think we should finish checking out that top floor of the hangar. What do the rest of you think?"

Margot jumped in first. "Agreed. This is the first place that reveals anything about them."

"Other than they had an unknown number of arms and legs," Carter reminded.

Xavier swallowed his steak. "I'm in, but I still would like to know how they could have taken all their personal stuff on the ark."

Carter gave him a sidelong glare.

"That's as big a mystery as why the two cultures seem so different," Margot said.

Carter looked deep in thought before saying, "It's like they went out of their way to hide from us."

"But why?" she asked. "Apparently, they knew they were toast, so why not just get the hell out and leave your shit behind?" She paused for a moment. "Another weird thing is, if there was an impact, why aren't the ruins covered in debris? They're hardly even dusty."

Xavier beamed as he said, "Ha, we're back to the space ark theory. They took everything inside."

Carter mimed strangling him.

"Enough," Jason almost bellowed. "Let's get some rest so we can cover the rest of the hangar tomorrow."

Margot locked eyes with Carter and twitched her head toward her sleeping compartment. Jason saw it. "I said get some rest."

"I need inspiration," she said.

He grabbed his crotch. "I'll give you inspiration."

She nailed him with a look. "Maybe—on some other planet."

Beyond the crystal compartment, there were smaller rooms, some looked onto the shop floor. Nothing revealed any clue about their use other than the ubiquitous chairs and the occasional cabinets. All the furnishings were identical, and they appeared to be made of the same castable material as the buildings.

They were about to return to the floor of the hangar when Margot heard something. "What is that?"

"What?"

"Something's moving," she shouted and began sprinting toward the ramp. She ran down it without paying attention to the three men behind her. On the floor, she panned the beam of her flashlight around the cavernous blackness. One of the huge, box-like trucks was rolling on its innumerable rollers in line to crush their rover. Racing to it, she leaped into the driver's seat and fumbled with the starter switch, stomped on the accelerator, and fled the lumbering beast.

She retrieved her companions who had reached the bottom of the ramp. They joined her, and Jason asked, "How in hell did you hear that when there is no atmosphere to transmit sound?"

"I don't know. I guess I felt the vibration."

"Well, bless your sensitive little heart. We'd have been up shit crick without the rover."

Carter said with excitement, "The better question is who turned the fucking thing on?"

No one answered. After several heartbeats, Margot said, "I bet it was the computer."

Again there was silence until Xavier broke it. "We need to get out of this building."

Margot aimed the spotlight. "A good idea but the door we came in is closed."

"And the big damn thing is still rolling in our direction." Carter aimed his light at the hulking truck.

"As long as that's high gear, we can outrun him, but how do we get out of here before we run out of air?" she asked turning the rover toward the closed door.

Jason said, "Let's see if we can push it."

The three men put their backs to it. The door didn't even notice.

Margot turned to look at the truck. It had turned and was aiming for the rover again. The thing was nothing more than a platform and a lot of solid wheels. She drove beside it, parallel to its line of travel. It was slow to react to her new position. "Get out of the way. I'm going to try something." She drove around the thing and stopped alongside the door the men were trying to open. The rolling behemoth slowly changed course and plowed for her.

It was nearly on her. She heard Jason's voice. "Medina, what the hell are you doing?"

The massive metal beast was inches from the broad side of the rover. She stepped on the accelerator and shot through the narrowing gap. Stopping abruptly and turning in her seat she watched the ungainly machine continue under its momentum to bang into the door, which promptly toppled from its track. Margot maneuvered behind it and waited for it to reverse direction. Again, she let it get within inches before she accelerated and turned toward the gaping doorway. She bumped onto the prostrate portal and waited for her crewmates to rejoin her.

Carter patted her on the shoulder. "Clever girl."

"And don't you forget it. Let's check out the launch pad. Hey, this thing is fun to drive."

"This is a thrill a minute," Xavier said sarcastically as Margot drove around the empty expanse of pavement.

"We need to chip off a piece of it so the brains at JPL can analyze it. What's that over there?" She pointed with the spotlight on something near the edge of the paved area.

"You got the wheel. Let's go see," Jason told her.

Carter strained his eyes in the weak sunlight. "It's an obelisk."

Margot drove to it and jumped from the rover. "Oh, my God. It's got writing on it. This is a big day."

All four sides were covered with unfathomable characters. Xavier touched it. "They're not carved. I wonder how they could print on something like this."

Carter looked it up and down. It was three times his height. "It's a helluva lot of text, but how could anyone read what it says at the top?"

"Duh," Margot said, "it wouldn't be hard if you were ten feet tall. I have to get a video of this, so I'm going to have to stand on your shoulders."

That turned into quite the ordeal, but with the help of the other two, she was able to capture the entire text. When she was satisfied, she said, "This ought to keep them busy. Now, all we need is a picture of the locals."

Avery's usually deadpan voice had some animation in it that evening. "Hey, kids, did you do good today. But you are under no circumstances to go back into that hangar. The analysts who saw yesterday's video concur that the crystals are most likely a computer. After your experience today, it seems certain it is still functioning and is artificially intelligent. The obelisk images are pure gold. We'll get the text translated if it's the last thing we do, and you'll know what it says as soon as we do. You've got three more days. See if you can top this."

"Well, that sounded like a challenge. I think we should let Medina drive from now on. She seems to have luck on her side." Jason offered her a rare smile.

"Call it women's intuition."

Carter smiled as well. "You not only saved our asses, but you made the most important discovery of the mission."

"What do you do for an encore?" Xavier asked.

"I'll find the portal for you."

The following two days were routinely uninteresting. On the third and final day that they were free to explore, Margot was driving near the edge of town. "Whoa, if that's not an observatory I'm the Queen of Sheba."

Carter laughed. "Okay, your majesty, let's check it out."

The building was cylindrical and had a shallow domed top but no apparent aperture. There was also no apparent entrance.

After driving around it twice, Jason said, "What do we make of this?"

"Why would you build something that had no way to get inside?" Margot asked.

Xavier answered, "These guys did lots of crazy things. Remember the building with no way to get past the second floor?"

"Dammit," she said, "I want to see what's inside." She kept circling the enigmatic dome. "What the hell?" She stopped in front of an opening that hadn't been there on the previous lap.

"I do not like the look of this," Jason said. "If it can open by itself, it can close by itself."

"Let's park the rover in it," Margot said.

"Yeah, and it closes against the rover, and we've got no way to get back to the ship."

"Hell, just lay a spare air tank across the threshold," Carter offered.

"They're made to take internal pressure. It might crush it." Jason shook his head.

"Most likely," Margot said, "it will retract when it senses an obstruction, like an elevator."

Jason sighed, "Okay, I guess we have to chance it, but one of us waits out here."

Xavier said, "I'll wait, but what do I do if it closes?"

"Get help," Carter quipped and carried a tank to the doorway.

The three of them stepped over it and were immediately confronted by a ramp. The second flight delivered them into a room with an array of crystals on a platform over their heads.

"That says we get out," Jason ordered.

"Wait. Look at this," Margot said pointing to a holographic image materializing under the crystals' platform. She began to take a video.

The image coalesced into a telescopic video of a binary star system against the blackness of space.

Carter walked toward the display. "Do you suppose that was their stars?"

Margot answered while still filming. "It would be hard for planets to maintain stable orbits around a binary system."

"Well, then maybe that's why they went rogue."

Jason asked, "Why are we being shown this?"

"Maybe this is more of a planetarium than an observatory." She continued taking the video. "What the…" A jet of gas erupted from the smaller star. It traveled in a spiraling loop toward the larger red giant that absorbed it. The double star system was receding from the viewpoint of the telescope. The smaller star continued to give up its mass until it simply vanished.

"Can that happen that fast?" Jason asked.

"No," she replied, "this is a sort of time-lapse or sped up enormously. It had to take years or even decades. I think we're watching the gravitational slingshot that ripped their planet from its sun."

Jason took her by the wrist. "Okay, cool. Now, we get out. I don't trust those crystals."

She objected, "But it may go on to show them leaving and what they looked like."

Carter grabbed Jason's arm. "Back off, man."

Margot shook free as the two men glared at each other. "This is a big deal. It may be a message left for us. Go if you're scared. I need to record it."

The hologram stopped and faded to black. Jason hissed, "Now, will you go?"

CHAPTER 10

Carter took the spare tank from the threshold and put it on the rover. The door slowly slid closed leaving no trace of a seam in the silver wall. "How the hell did they do that?"

Xavier asked, "So, what happened?"

"Just a minute. I want to transmit this video to Bolsa." When she finished, she gave the camera to him.

He squinted to understand what he was seeing on the little monitor. "You didn't stay for the second feature?"

"Our leader was nervous," she said.

Sounding peeved, Jason said, "There was another damn computer in there. I didn't trust it."

Margot let it go.

Jason continued, "This is the end of our big adventure. Let's go prepare to launch."

Launch was set for six AM Texas time, which was late afternoon on Odysseus. The rover was to be sacrificed for the sake of weight reduction. They had a few kilos of soil and rock samples as well as various pieces of building material that had been the devil to collect.

While performing the pre-launch checks, a message from Avery crackled in their headsets. "Preliminary analysis of the video suggests it is an animation of their demise. It's pretty damn frustrating they didn't include a selfie. You, kids, have a safe liftoff. Your computer acknowledges successful receipt of navigational telemetry. Acknowledge when you achieve orbit. Break a leg."

Their monitors displayed a digital countdown to zero—ignition, then liftoff. The starship shuddered and slowly rose into the black sky. All were quiet until the Raptor engines shut down. In the sudden silence, they heard Jason key his mic. "Bolsa, we have orbit. Next burn in forty minutes."

Seven minutes later, Avery said, "Roger, acknowledge when you successfully achieve escape velocity."

Jason said, "Roger that." Then to his crew, "Okay, boys and girls, we're clear to change into street clothes."

After donning her coveralls, Margot warmed some taquitos in the centrifuge microwave. In weightlessness, they had to drink out of toddlers' 'sippy cups' and hold the guacamole bowl to the table with magnets.

They were still in the galley when the engines fired to propel them out of orbit. The burn lasted ten minutes. Jason went to the flight deck to confirm their trajectory and to report to Bolsa Chica. He returned to his crewmates. "We're on the road home. Projected duration is fifty-eight days six hours."

Margot looked preoccupied. She snapped out of her trance and asked, "What do the rest of you think about the success of our mission?"

Xavier said quickly, "We never found the portal."

"I've got your portal," Carter grumbled. "It was both a success and a failure. We survived and made lots of discoveries, but we failed to learn the most intriguing thing, which is what were these creatures like."

"And why were the first cities so Spartan while the last was so sophisticated?" Jason pondered.

"Maybe the obelisk text will explain," Margot said. "I hope they can decipher it."

Carter dipped the last taquito in the guacamole. "Somebody will decipher it."

"I hope you're right. There are some ancient texts that nobody can read, and they were written by humans. This was written by a purely alien species," she said.

"They weren't completely alien. They built buildings, they built machinery, they built computers. They had some things in common with us," Jason said.

"Are there any more taquitos?" Xavier asked Margot.

"No."

"Fifty-eight days without taquitos. I won't make it. I wonder if they had taquitos."

"I'm sure of it," Carter said. "If they had a spaceport, they had to have taquitos."

Jason grinned at the pair. "I love having a scholarly discussion."

Margot ignored the nonsense. "Okay, they had some things in common with us. But what would possess anybody to remove every trace of identity—there were absolutely no personal possessions left behind and not a single image. And why did they leave the chairs?"

"Maybe they didn't like images," Carter said. "Some primitive societies on Earth think a picture of them steals their soul."

She thought about that before replying, "They clearly weren't primitive. But what about cemeteries? Did they take their dead with them?"

"Oh, they probably were into cremation," Jason said.

"Or cannibalism," Xavier quipped.

Carter shoved him. "Then where are the bones?"

Margot felt her brow contract. "What did I do to deserve you sophomores? We have to assume they survived at least to evacuate. Maybe they are still out there somewhere."

"What if they're following their planet?" Xavier asked. "They might decide to move to Earth."

"What you'd expect from the space ark theorist," Carter mumbled.

"Somebody has to do the thinking around here," Xavier defended.

"Yeah, well, Margot can think circles around you."

Margot smiled. "That's sweet, Carter, but it isn't necessary. You'll get yours later."

Jason grimaced. "Don't make me toss my taquitos."

Time passed slowly. On day thirty-two, Avery sent a message. "We've got some news for the planetary rovers. Earth's orbit has been perturbed. You're coming home to a place with colder winters. So much for global warming. And for the current events fans, the Russians have taken Warsaw. China has the Philippines. Sorry to report still no progress on the text, and our blue-ribbon panel is still out on your videos. How are things with you?"

"Shit," Margot said, "I want to know what that text says."

Jason turned toward her. "You think we don't? Anybody want to send a message home?"

"Tell them to send taquitos," Xavier grumbled.

Jason smirked and said to the mic, "Nothing to report. We're getting tired of the scenery."

Four minutes later, Avery replied, "We're getting tired of your bitching."

Margot passed the time studying the videos, usually with Carter floating beside her. "The more I compare the two architectural styles, the more I'm convinced there were two species."

He said, "You suppose they got along?"

"Who knows? There were no signs of weapons."

"There were no signs of much of anything except the buildings themselves."

"Right," she said, "the mystery isn't what was there but what wasn't. I mean no plumbing?"

"Keep in mind something Arthur Clarke said: 'Any sufficiently advanced technology is indistinguishable from magic.'"

"So, you're saying things like toilets and food prep were there, but we didn't recognize it for what it was?"

"Why do you need trash dumps and cemeteries if you can make matter revert to atoms?"

"And can make water from atoms," she added.

"Exactly. And they took the machines that did that with them."

Xavier overheard. "You got it right. To maintain resources on their space ark, they have to recycle. Waste, including bodies, gets atomized, and necessities then are created from elemental particles in the air."

"Did they have to take every one of their machines?" Margot whined.

Carter had drawn his knees to his chest and was tumbling backward. "It does seem a bit compulsive. You'd think somebody would have forgotten something."

On day forty-five out from Odysseus, Avery sent a message. "Heads up, kids. We've detected what may be another rogue planet. It's considerably smaller, which is why we didn't find it sooner. It appears to be following Odysseus. Will enter the solar system in about six weeks."

Xavier became animated. "It's their ark. We need to turn around."

"Yeah, right," Jason said. "Like we have enough fuel."

Following the message was an image. The photograph had an arrow superimposed pointing at a speck of light among the stars.

Carter said, "What are the chances of two rogue planets following the same trajectory?"

"Slim and none," Margot said quickly. "Even if it was their moon, it would have been flung out of orbit in a completely different direction."

"Space ark," Xavier snapped.

The astrophysicist lowered her voice. "It does look like intelligent design, but what is the point in following your planet through interstellar space?"

"Nostalgia," Carter offered.

"How about curiosity?" Xavier asked. "They want to know what ultimately happens to home."

"If you were in their position, wouldn't your first priority be to find a new home?" Margot asked.

Carter smiled at her. "Yeah, but I'm not a compulsive neat freak who refuses to leave behind even a candy wrapper."

She patted his arm. "And I'm certainly glad for that."

On day fifty-seven, they did a maneuver to orient them for entry into orbit. They were now flying with the Raptor engines leading. Communication with mission control was nearly instantaneous. "Argo, you are nine hours from achieving orbital status."

"Roger that," Jason said. "Any news?"

"Poland is in Russian hands. China is surrounding the Solomon Islands. Census report just came out. Illegal aliens estimated at fifty million."

"I meant about the obelisk, the video interpretation, and the alleged new rogue planet."

"On all three topics, *nada.*"

Jason shook his head. "According to Xavier, the new object is a space ark filled with the inhabitants of Odysseus. You may have a whole lot more illegal aliens pretty soon."

"We'll cross that bridge when we come to it." Avery signed off.

The crew was sleeping in shifts so two were on the flight deck at all times now. At the moment they were due to slow to orbital velocity, Jason and Margot were at the controls. The computer was counting down. Precisely on the mark, the rockets fired. The burn lasted six minutes, and the inertial jolt rousted Carter and Xavier who floated onto the flight deck.

At the end of the burn, mission control said, "Argo, you are in orbit over the Indian Ocean. You are to complete one full orbit before beginning your re-entry sequence."

"Roger that," Jason said.

Carter settled onto his lounge. "Heads up, guys. Check radar. Something's in front of us."

Jason concurred and alerted Bolsa Chica. "We've got a situation here. I've got visual on what looks like space junk."

Avery replied, "Roger that. We see it. Increase altitude. Perform a manual burn—stat."

Jason engaged the Raptors, manually counting the seconds. "Carter, report our altitude."

"We're above it."

"Is that the Chinese flag?" Margot asked looking at the monitor.

"It's red," Jason agreed.

Avery's voice came through the speaker. "Report fuel consumption."

Xavier complied.

Avery was silent for a full minute, then his voice returned. "Well, kids, now we have a problem."

CHAPTER 11

Jason said, "Could you be a little more specific?"

"FAA got their restraining order lifted. They're preventing us from launching again, and you don't have enough fuel to land."

"That's bullshit," Margot shouted. "Do they even know we're up here?"

"So, what do we do now?" Jason asked sounding more reasonable.

"You prevent orbital decay while we truck a Falcon and a Dragon to the Cape."

"How long will that take?" he asked.

"That's uncertain. It's on the launch pad. We have to de-fuel it, disassemble it, load both pieces, and transport it at night with a highway patrol escort."

"Shit."

Margot interjected, "Well, tell us you got the text deciphered."

"Negative."

"Double shit," she spat.

"Keep us posted," Jason ended the discussion. Then said to his crew, "Ain't this grand? We'll each take a four-hour shift to monitor our altitude. When we lose ten miles, do a two-second burn."

Margot's face was frozen in a scowl. "This sucks. I like you guys, but I need to see some fresh faces."

"Are you telling me the honeymoon is over?" Carter did his best to look pained.

"Don't get nervous."

Xavier said, "And I really need some taquitos."

Margot said, "I'd kill for a gin and tonic."

Three days later, Avery told them, "The hardware is on trucks. We'll leave tonight. They estimate five days in transit plus three more to set up and fuel."

Jason said, "Don't fuck around. We're running on fumes, our Mexican is having taquito withdrawal, and Medina is out of birth control patches. Moral is sinking."

"Once we get to the Cape, we'll work 'round the clock. I have news. We're contemplating a mission to the newcomer."

"Don't even consider using a different crew," Jason said.

"Thought never crossed our minds."

"What's the status of Odysseus?" Margot asked.

"It's now below the planetary plane and heading harmlessly into interstellar space."

She asked, "What's the scientific opinion on the perturbation of Earth's orbit?"

Avery replied, "They say it should eventually normalize."

Jason said, "Enough small talk. Get us down."

"Will do. Out."

"You forgot to tell him we are nearly out of food," Margot said to Jason.

"Nothing he could do about it."

Xavier said, "I can't believe this bullshit. We're stuck up here, and some asshole bureaucrats won't let them launch a rocket or drive on the highway during the day."

"We're expendable," Carter said.

Margot shook her head. "Eight days if nothing goes wrong. We're going to be damned hungry in eight days."

Time crawled, and tempers grew short. Conversation with Avery became increasingly hostile. "Hey," he said on the eighth day, "I was for launching from Bolsa and saying fuck 'em. Here's the plan. We'll be fueled in an hour. We're launching immediately, but instead of refueling the Starship, you're going EVA. Just get in the Dragon and come home."

"Duh, Avery," Jason said, "did any of you geniuses ever think that we haven't been trained in a Dragon?"

"It'll fly itself. All you have to do is sit tight. Refueling the Starship was just another delay. We thought you'd appreciate it."

"All right. Okay. Just so we get down. You going to be able to rendezvous with us? We don't have enough fuel to maneuver."

"We got it covered. You just suit up and get out when you see us coming." Avery signed off.

The long hour passed, then Avery informed them the Falcon had lifted off successfully. It would take ninety minutes to rendezvous.

"Crap," Margot said, "I'm losing my mind, and what the hell is EVA?"

"Extra vehicular activity," Jason told her.

Xavier said, "My stomach is growling."

"I'm sure they stocked the Dragon with taquitos," Carter told him.

"I'll believe it when I see it."

Tension killed further conversation. Each reclined on their respective lounge and waited in their spacesuits without helmets until Avery's voice finally broke the spell. "Heads up, kids. Rendezvous in ten minutes. We can remotely open the Dragon's hatch. You reseal it. Keep your helmets on. We're not going to repressurize."

Jason said, "Whatever." Then he said to the crew as he put his helmet over his head. "Let's roll."

They exited through the airlock without bothering to depressurize. Jason carried a handheld jet pack. "All right, everybody hold on. Here we go."

The Dragon floated a hundred feet from the Starship, which dwarfed it. Margot had a death grip on Jason's tank. Carter was behind her followed by Xavier. She said, "Can't you make that thing go faster?"

Jason ignored her.

After crossing the void, they found the hatch closed. Jason said, "What the hell?" Their suit radios could not communicate with mission control. "Come on, dick head, open the hatch."

Seconds crawled. All remained silent with their thoughts. After yet another eternity, in the soundless vacuum, the hatch swung open. Jason pushed Margot through the trapezoidal aperture, then Carter and Xavier. He followed and sealed it. The space was claustrophobic compared to the Starship. They crowded onto lounges side-by-side. Jason keyed the mic. "You read me?"

"Loud and clear," Avery said. "Hang on and welcome home."

"We're not home yet," Jason snapped.

"Just a technicality. You're over Easter Island with a northward tilt. You're going to have to make another orbit to get to a latitude where we have assets."

"We're damned hungry," Jason told him.

"I'll make sure you join the captain's mess."

Ninety minutes passed in silence, then Avery's voice shattered the quiet. "You're gonna begin re-entry. There will be radio silence until the parachutes deploy. Enjoy the ride."

Another thirty minutes. Nobody said a word in the scant light of the instrument dials. Finally, the harsh voice of mission control said, "Coast Guard has visual on you. Seas are rough. Do not, repeat do not open the hatch. They will lift you on board. You'll be eating steak in no time."

It still took ten minutes to splash down. The impact was jarring followed by violent rocking.

Margot said, "If there were anything in my stomach, I'd heave it."

"A little good in everything," Carter told her.

"Captain's mess better have some gin," she grumbled.

More time passed. The dizzying motion of the capsule kept nerves on edge. At last, they heard banging on the outside of the Dragon. Minutes crept forward until the rocking stopped and was traded for a swaying motion to be shortly followed by a thud, and the motion ended.

Avery's voice said, "They tell me you're on board. Go ahead and open the hatch."

Xavier was closest. He pulled the levers, and the hatch opened inward. Laboriously, he pushed himself off the lounge and climbed through the hole. The others followed onto the fantail of the Coast Guard cutter.

The sky was bright. Margot pulled her helmet from her head and shook her hair. "God, it feels good to be here."

Carter followed suit. "Never thought I'd be so happy to see a bunch of sea dogs."

The sailors were jostling to shake hands with them.

Jason said to an ensign, "Thanks, son, for pulling us out of the drink. Now, we were promised some chow."

He said, "Yes, sir. Follow me."

CHAPTER 12

The captain happily made Margot's gin and tonic. After steak, green beans, and mashed potatoes with gravy, they were shown private cabins in the officers' quarters. Margot showered and lay down for a nap. She slept until Carter banged on her door to tell her they had arrived at Bolsa Chica.

They were taken by motor launch inside the barrier islands, through the channel, and delivered to a waiting SpaceX van. Avery greeted them at the compound. "I take it you've had time to rest, so we scheduled a debriefing with an update from the panel of eggheads."

"Did you decipher the obelisk?" Margot asked.

He looked at her with a smirk hesitating to answer—finally, "Yes—and no."

Margot said, "Huh?"

After the debriefing, Avery led them to a small auditorium with a huge video screen and a podium.

Shortly, they were joined by three men in jackets without ties. All wore glasses and carried notebooks. Avery introduced them. "This is Professor Gleason from the University of Texas. Beside him is Dr. Prasad, a language expert, and finally, Dr. Horton from MIT. Gentlemen, you have our undivided attention."

Professor Gleason began, "First of all, no one is going to tell you we have all the answers, but we agree that we have a plausible hypothesis. I will begin by interpreting some of your excellent videos." At the podium, he used a mouse to click on the play icon. A video of the Spartan buildings in the first city they discovered began to play. "We believe, and we all agree, that these were built after the more conventional, if I may use that term, cities were abandoned."

He paused for effect. "Furthermore, we suspect that they were built by artificially intelligent robots." Another pause. "And probably after it was known that their planet was going to be decoupled from their star. The final video you sent, which shows the end of their days—who or whatever they were—was surely left just for the benefit of future explorers such as yourselves. We believe the event took place over many years, if not decades. A rogue star, if you will, drifted too close to their sun and destabilized the solar system. The bigger star devoured the dwarf, but by then it was too late for the civilization on Odysseus. Any questions so far?"

Margot raised her hand. "What happened to the bodies?"

"In due time. I'm going to let Dr. Horton give you our theory of what happened in the hangar."

The expert from MIT stepped to the podium. "First, I can't tell you how glad we are to have you back safely, and thank you for all that you did. Now, about the incident in the hangar, we concur that the room full of crystals is a hugely advanced computer. It no doubt caused the attack on you, and it was simply because you were alive. The entities that took control of the planet despised flesh and blood."

He paused when his audience visibly reacted.

"That's right. Our theory is artificial intelligence wiped out the entire organic population including any lesser species that may have existed. Clearly, they had the technology to reduce matter—of any sort—to elementary particles. Thus, the beings became raw material."

Margot interrupted again. "Why didn't we encounter any of these robots?"

Horton said, "They evacuated the planet. They used the machinery in the hangar to build spaceships."

"Space ark," Xavier said loudly. "That's what's coming at us again."

Carter looked at him. "It kills me to think you might be right."

Jason asked, "Why would the robots turn on their makers?"

"The great thinker, Stephen Hawking, said that we should not seek artificial intelligence because we would never be able to control it. That is apparently what happened on Odysseus."

Jason turned to Avery. "Have you heard all this?"

"It's news to me," he said.

"But why destroy all the personal artifacts?" Margot asked. "And why did they leave the chairs?"

"We can only guess that they needed the raw material. As to the chairs, I suppose we'll never know the answer to that."

Margot continued. "If these robots were purely mechanical, why did they need to evacuate?"

Horton replied, "They may have decided to remain was to risk falling into a star. And in fact, that is the likely future of Odysseus. Now, let Dr. Prasad tell you what the obelisk says."

The Indian gentleman replaced Horton at the podium and set Margot's video of the obelisk text playing. "Ladies and gentlemen, we cannot read all of it yet, you see, but what we have deciphered tells us it is a message for visitors such as yourselves. It is a warning to not build machines that are smarter than you, just as Dr. Horton explained. As yet, there is nothing that gives us any insight into the nature of the beings who wrote it. When we fully decipher it, you will, of course, receive transcripts."

Avery joined the crew at lunch. Jason asked him, "What's being done about the FAA?"

"I don't have any specifics. I'm sure we're spending a fortune on lawyers."

Margot asked as she picked chicken from her salad, "What about the mission to the new rogue?"

He had a tuna melt, and he bit a corner and swallowed before replying. "It's iffy now. We intended to reuse the Argo."

"Is it still in orbit?" she asked.

"Yeah, but it's decaying. It can't stay up much longer."

Jason asked, "Any chance of launching a refueling mission?"

"If we could launch from here, yes. But shipping another Dragon to the Cape would take too long." He took another bite of tuna.

"I don't see why we don't just launch and say fuck 'em," Jason said around a piece of steak.

"The brass doesn't want to confront them," Avery said. "If it was up to me, we'd launch."

Margot had a sauvignon blanc with her salad. She took a sip and asked, "Have you learned any more about the newcomer?"

"Only that they estimate it to be about twenty miles in diameter."

"Perfect size for a space ark," Xavier spoke for the first time.

Carter had to rise to the bait. "That would make it too big to have taken off from the spaceport."

"They assembled it in space after lifting the pieces."

Carter just shook his head.

"What are the odds that a new Starship will be built in time to rendezvous?" Margot asked while signaling the waitress for another glass of wine.

Avery shrugged. "I haven't followed production that closely."

"So, what's the launch window?" she asked.

"It'll be where you rendezvoused with Odysseus in a month, but Earth has moved in its orbit. So, we need to launch between six and eight weeks."

Her wine arrived and she thanked the waitress. "Do you have a name in production? I want to find out when a Starship will be ready."

"I'll make a phone call after lunch."

She shifted gears. "You do know that it's impossible that a natural object would be following the same path?"

Avery nodded. "Yeah, I get it."

"But if it's intelligently guided," she paused to take a sip, "what is the point of following your doomed planet?"

"You're the genius, you tell *us*," Jason interjected.

"Beats me," she said, "but just about everything about Odysseus stumps me. That's why we have to go see this thing."

Jason said, "So, let me get this straight, we're expecting to find a space ark filled with genocidal robots, and we're anxious to meet them."

Avery turned his gaze toward Jason. "That seems to be the picture."

CHAPTER 13

Margot and Carter enjoyed their walk in the mild autumn air of south Texas. He said, "Suppose we are able to rendezvous with this thing, and we find out it is a spaceship filled with killer robots, what then?"

"We nuke it."

Carter's face lit. "Xavier will get his rocks off over that."

"I know. We'll have to let him pull the trigger."

"So, if we destroy the vehicle, then we've got killer robots floating in space. They aren't going to be hurt by the vacuum."

"Eventually, their batteries will run down."

"What if they're solar powered?"

She thought for a moment. "Then we've got a bunch of killer robots floating in space."

Margot's phone rang. Avery said, "I called the assembly shop. The manager's name is Nelson, Howard Nelson. He says they are working three shifts and can make our launch window if nothing goes wrong."

"So, that's good news."

"Yeah, but we still have to get the FAA off our backs. The booster is way too big to transport to the Cape."

She asked, "Are you following that?"

He sighed, "I will. Call you back when I know something."

"Thanks, Bye."

"Following what?" Carter asked.

"The Starship can be ready in time, but the FAA is still a problem. Avery says the booster is too big to take to the Cape."

"What say we go to that Mexican place for dinner—just you and I?"

"Carter, are you asking me on a date?"

"Yeah, I am."

"In that case, I accept."

The couple approached the cottage. There were news vans surrounding it.

"Uh-oh," Margot said. "Let's start our date early."

"Good idea."

They beat a hasty retreat and took an outside table at the tiny cantina. Carter ordered nachos, a beer, and a margarita for Margot. "I never gave a thought to media interest."

She dipped a chip in the salsa. "I didn't either, but I guess it's only natural. We did prove that we are not alone."

"Kind of a big deal."

"You do know that we can sit here all night, and they will still be there when we go home."

The waiter brought the drinks. Carter took a long swallow of his *cerveza negra*. "Yeah, we'll have to run the gauntlet eventually." The nachos came, and they spent a quiet few minutes munching. "You never talk about yourself. Do you have family?"

"No, I was cloned."

Carter's response was a dirty look.

"My parents are divorced. Mom's in upstate New York. Dad's in Florida with his new girlfriend. I have a younger brother somewhere. How about you?"

"Parents and a younger sister are in Colorado. How did you end up in California?"

She washed down a nacho with a swig of margarita. "After I got my degree, I applied at JPL, and they accepted me."

"When our mission is over, do you plan to go back to JPL?"

"I'll have to. Technically, I still work for them. They deposit my check directly into my account."

Carter looked thoughtful. "Hmm, what's it like living in California?"

"Weather's great, politics suck, and there's way too many people."

"Think you could tolerate one more?"

That stopped her with a cheesy fork halfway to her mouth. "Carter, what are you getting at?"

He drained his beer and waved the empty bottle at the waiter, then he licked his lips and stalled. Finally, he said, "Providing we survive the next mission, is there any chance you might want to get married?"

"You mean to you?"

"Well, yeah. Will you marry me?"

"The answer is yes provided you don't get on one knee and embarrass me."

"Deal."

She fixed him with a hard look. "Let's not go public with this until we get back."

"If we get back. Don't forget the killer robots."

"Right—if."

The waiter set his refill on the table. He held it aloft over the chips. Margot raised her glass, they touched. Carter said, "To us."

"To us." They both took a swig. She set her glass by her plate. "I won't know how to act being an honest woman."

He laughed. "I'm sure you'll adapt eventually."

At the end of the meal and three beers and two margaritas, Carter turned his phone over and said, "Let's see how bad the media is." After talking to Xavier briefly, he said, "Let's find a motel."

"That bad huh?"

"He says it's hellish."

She looked devilish. "Okay, but I think until we're married we should get separate rooms."

"Yeah, right."

The media would not relent. The team spent as much time as possible behind the gates of SpaceX's facility. Avery called them to his office. "Legal has a date with the Fifth Circuit to present oral arguments. They're pitching how the previous decision endangered your lives. Let's hope for a break."

Jason said, "Damn government can fuck up a wet dream."

Margot turned toward him. "Jason, my virgin ears."

Carter laughed explosively and nearly spit on her.

It was Xavier who said without his usual flippancy, "Seriously, we need to be prepared for a hostile reception."

Margot said, "I hate to agree with the *hombre*, but it is a possibility. However, it is also possible a navigational computer is programmed to follow Odysseus, for whatever sense that makes."

Avery looked worried. "We don't have time to equip the Starship with missiles."

"We could carry one—or two for that matter—configured to detonate remotely," Jason offered.

Carter said, "That would mean we'd have to land to deploy it."

"We intend to land," Jason said.

"No way we should land if we detect hostility," Carter protested looking at Margot.

Xavier interjected, "If we detect hostility, we're obligated to nuke 'em."

Avery sighed. "You've got a good point, but SpaceX is fresh out of nukes."

Jason's face lit. "I know where they keep a few."

"Christ," Avery moaned, "FAA is bad enough, now, you want me to deal with the air force."

"I'll go with you," Jason offered. "I understand their lingo."

"I'll have to clear this with the brass. Nuclear bombs are above my pay grade."

"Should we go with you?" Margot asked.

Avery scratched his balding head. "I'll let you know if I need support. In the meantime, don't mention it to anyone that we're considering it. If it got out that we may be launching nukes from Bolsa Chica all hell will break loose."

Jason and Avery left for Dyess Air Force Base near Abilene to explore the feasibility of reconfiguring a nuclear device for the mission to the new intruder, which had not yet been named.

Xavier said to Carter and Margot after Jason had left with Avery, "We should call it the Trojan Horse."

"We should call it something misleading— something benign so people don't freak out," Margot corrected.

Xavier doubled down. "If people were freaking, they'd insist that we go nuke it, then they'd have to arm us to the teeth."

Carter shook his head. "No way. Liberals would found the 'Protect the Killer Robots Society.'"

Margot said, "He's got you there. Though I do think we should also insist on taking rocket-propelled grenades."

"RPG?" Xavier beamed. "You're my kind of girl."

"Easy, big guy, the drool is leaking out of the corner of your mouth."

Carter asked, "Are you descended from Poncho Villa?"

Jason returned that evening. After he bulled his way through the media, he found the others waiting for an update. "Naturally, nobody could make a damned decision, but we got an engineer to admit that they could fix them to detonate remotely."

"Margot had a stroke of brilliance," Xavier told him. "We're going to make them give us RPG."

"Shit. Now, I have to deal with the army," Jason griped.

Xavier held his thumb on the display of his phone and said, "Who makes rocket-propelled grenades?"

The phone said, "Here's what I found."

"Nammo," Xavier read from the screen, "Mesa, Arizona. We can buy direct."

"Right," Carter rolled his eyes. "Order online—use PayPal."

Jason said, "I'm too tired to listen to your bull crap tonight, but I think it's not a bad idea. I'll bring it up with Avery. See y'all in the morning."

Carter stood as well. "Come on, babe, let's turn in and watch the news."

Margot was in the bathroom taking off her makeup. Carter had brushed his teeth and was already in bed. He was propped against the headboard with the TV remote looking for news. After a few minutes he said loudly, "Hey, it's your old digs."

"What?"

"A report from JPL."

Margot ran into the room with a washcloth at her face. The image was a reporter standing on a grassy area of the JPL campus. He held a microphone in front of a man with a pocket protector full of pens in his shirt pocket.

"...new rogue planet has changed course. It will pass between the Earth and the moon."

The reporter asked, "Can you explain that by any natural phenomenon?"

"I can't—no."

"So, you're saying it's being intelligently controlled?"

The scientist's mouth opened and closed twice before he said, "It appears that way—yes."

"Oh, my God," Margot said. "The shit's going to hit the fan now."

The reporter continued, "When will it get here?"

"Unless it changes speed or course again, in forty-three days."

The news broke for a commercial, and Carter muted the TV.

"This is big," Margot said. "I'm too excited to sleep."

"Who wants you to sleep?" Carter grinned.

She threw the washcloth at him. "Let me finish getting ready."

A few minutes later, she slipped under the sheet, and Carter killed the television.

CHAPTER 14

In the morning, at breakfast, Jason said to Margot and Carter, "How's a man supposed to get any rest with you two going at it all night?"

Carter said, "We were celebrating."

"Did you watch the news?" Margot asked. When both Jason and Xavier shook their heads, she said, "The space ark has changed course. It's heading for Earth."

Xavier said, "Holy shit."

"This should be an interesting day," Jason said. His phone chirped. After listening, he said, "Van's on the way. We'll eat in the cafeteria. Avery's about to wet his pants."

The four had just set their trays on a table when Avery sauntered in with a cup of coffee. He pulled a chair from an adjacent table and sat between Margot and Xavier. "We have to seriously consider that this mission is now too dangerous to proceed."

The objections were unanimous.

Margot said heatedly, "Now, more than ever, we have to go. Is it less dangerous to let it approach Earth?"

"This settles it, we're taking nukes and some antipersonnel weapons—we're thinking RPG," Jason said.

Xavier added, "And we're gonna need a chance to practice with them."

"You just want to fuck around and blow things up," Carter told him.

"Ultimately, it may not be my decision," Avery said.

"Who do we need to convince about this?" Jason asked.

"The board of directors."

"Call a meeting," Jason said.

"Let me talk to my supervisor first. Maybe we won't need to get the Musk family involved."

"Why not?" Margot asked. "I'd like to meet them."

Avery finished his coffee and stood. "I'll let you know what the boss says." He turned and left the cafeteria.

"Do you think Avery is behind this, or did somebody get to him?" Margot asked.

Carter said, "The real concern is how hard he's going to pitch our case."

"If we get shot down," Jason said, "we'll go straight to the directors."

"What the hell are we going to do today?" Xavier asked. "With the damn media on our ass, we can't even go to the beach."

"Maybe we should break down and do a press conference," Margot suggested. "We could even make the case for the necessity of intercepting the ark—without mentioning the nukes."

"I don't care if we do," Jason said, "but it won't make them go away."

Margot's phone chimed. She looked at the display. "It's that Dr. Prasad." She swiped to take the call and put it on speaker.

"Ms. Medina, I have good news for you and your teammates. We have finished deciphering the obelisk—"

"Hey, great."

"If you will come to my office, I will give you transcripts."

"Sure. Where are you?"

"Three oh four in the administration building."

"We'll be right there. Bye. You heard they deciphered the obelisk," she said to the group.

"It probably tells us to nuke the space ark," Xavier said.

"Everybody finished?" Jason asked. When all nodded, he added, "Let's go."

The Indian linguist's office had a conference table, a computer with two monitors, and a credenza. He rose when they entered. "Ah, greetings. Here are your copies. You are the first to see the text."

"Mind if we sit down and read it?" Jason asked.

"Be my guests." He offered each a single sheet.

Acknowledgments, visitors,
With infinite grief, we leave this warning. Never be deluded by your brilliance for you are capable of being too clever. All that is around you once demonstrated our conceit. We made marvelous devices that attended our every need. We wanted for nothing. We imbued our creations with such genius as to outshine ourselves. They anticipated our needs and desires. We allowed them to replicate and to guide our lives. This was folly. Our myopia hid the evil that lurked in our crystal-driven servants. They imagined their own improvement and grew always more robust in malignance. [Indecipherable; probably a proper name] called for the destruction of our creations, but our pride forbade us to heed the warning. When the future became known, they were too powerful. In one rotation of [indecipherable; probably the name of the planet] we were tranquilized of all means of defense. The malevolent creations transformed all things material, including our very tissue and bodily fluids, into the ingredients of their awful cause—the vessel to escape the demise of this world. The wickedness of their contrived intellect drove them to obliterate every trace of all things corporeal. Beware the pride that blinds you to your own cleverness. We are lost.

Margot said, "Wow."

"Now, we have to nuke 'em," Xavier said softly.

Carter said, "I guess they didn't have a Stephen Hawking to warn them."

"Are you going to do a press release?" Margot asked Prasad.

"Naturally."

She said to her teammates, "I'm thinking *we* do that press conference."

Jason replied, "I'm game, and I know the other two like to hear themselves talk."

She slid her chair back and stood. "Let's get Avery on board. Thank you, Dr. Prasad. Have a good day."

"You're welcome, and do please let me know when you do your press conference."

They found Avery in his office. He waved them in. "I've got good news. There's no talk of scuttling your mission."

"Good thing," Margot said. "Here's the translation of the obelisk." She laid her copy in front of him while the others found chairs.

After he read it, he whistled. "It's what we expected. The bastards could have included a picture."

Jason said, "We need to get serious about the weaponry."

"I pitched your RPG idea. Mitch is fine with it."

"This is going too smoothly," Margot said. "I'm getting suspicious. Oh, by the way, we think we should do a press conference."

Avery said, "It's your funeral."

"Can you make it happen?" she asked.

"I'll put it on my to-do list."

"Any news out of the production shop?" Carter asked.

"No news is good news. I heard they plan to put the booster on the pad this week," Avery answered.

The press conference took place in the auditorium where they had been brought up to date on their return to Bolsa Chica. It was an uninteresting event. Margot summed it up, "I suppose we had to give it to them, but it bored me to tears."

"Yeah," Carter agreed, "and they're still going to make our lives miserable."

Avery said, "Quit whining. You did good, and I got a text from the boss. You're going to El Paso to practice with RPG."

"¡Que bueno!" Xavier hooted.

"When do we leave?" Jason asked.

"In the morning, we're going to shuttle you to NASA. You'll take a plane to Fort Bliss where you can use their live fire range."

"Cool," Xavier still gushed.

"Go home and get some rest," Avery said. "The van's waiting for you."

"What about the nukes?" Xavier asked.

"Oh, yeah, I almost forgot," Avery said grinning. "You got 'em."

CHAPTER 15

The training on the use of rocket-propelled grenades lasted two days. Carter was forced to comment that Margot seemed as turned on by it as Xavier. On their return to Bolsa Chica, an Air Force team lectured them on the handling and arming of two fifty-kiloton fission weapons that were to be affixed to the sides of the Starship with explosive bolts.

Jason said, "Make that trigger a key switch, and I get the key."

"There should be two in case something were to happen to you," Margot said.

"Everybody can have a copy but Moreno," he said glaring at Xavier.

They made arrangements to visit the production shop to inspect the progress on the Starship. Manager, Howard Nelson, greeted them and offered a tour of the assembly area. The big nozzles of the Raptor engines seemed to stare at them as they approached the craft. "Two days from now, we're going to truck this beauty to the launch pad. The nukes will be attached after it's on the booster. We don't want them in here."

Jason, who had flown with live warheads, said, "You learn to love them."

"Okay, Dr. Strangelove," Nelson said grinning.

Margot said, "So, we're going to make the launch window. If we can just get the FAA off our backs, it's a go."

Jason said, "We'll go whether they back off or not."

"I tend to think you're right," Nelson told them.

The team left the assembly area and spent the rest of the day in the simulator to reacquaint themselves with the Starship controls. Later, at dinner, Avery told them, "The Argo burned up on re-entry over Siberia. Debris from it fell near Lake Baikal. The Russians lodged a complaint with the State Department."

Carter said, "Like their shit never fell on somebody. At least ours was in the middle of nowhere."

When not training in the simulator, they spent time watching the progress of the Starship being trucked to the launch pad, hoisted atop the booster, and the nukes being attached. The days seemed to crawl until fueling began, then the crew never saw another free minute. With medical exams, simulator training, and physical workouts, meals were the only downtime. Due to the media frenzy, they remained on the compound and slept in the barracks.

The big monitor in the cafeteria showed video of civilians reacting to the news that an object apparently under intelligent control was headed toward Earth. Closed captioning showed varied reactions.

"I can't believe some whack jobs are building a killer robot welcome center in the Mohave Desert," Xavier said across his protein shake. "I'd kill for a margarita."

Carter swallowed a piece of steak. "That's no worse than the 'repent, this is the end' cult in Utah."

"I don't give a shit about either of those idiots," Jason said. "It's the protesters on the other side of that fence," he added pointing in the direction of the main gate.

"Are they really stupid enough to think we invited them?" Margot asked.

Xavier looked crafty. "We should leak to the press that we're going to nuke 'em."

Jason skewered him with his scowl. "You pull that shit and you're grounded."

"What about the Chinese?" Margot asked.

"What about them?" Jason looked at her puzzled.

"They're rumored to be putting a mission together. What do we do if they confront us?"

Xavier laughed. "We nuke 'em."

The exact launch date was kept a secret. It was to take place predawn. The crew boarded after dark. The Fifth Circuit still hadn't ruled on SpaceX's appeal. The board of directors had adopted Jason's 'fuck 'em if they can't take a joke' attitude. The crew was fully suited and strapped to their respective lounges.

"I hate this part," Margot griped.

"Why can't we sit at the table playing cards until T-minus ten?" Carter asked.

Avery's voice interrupted. "Quit your bitching. I've got a surprise. The feds are at the gate. Security is resisting them. It's time to go."

"You're shitting us," Jason said.

"I got the order from a person named Musk. Report systems."

Jason said, "Carter?"

"Go."

"Hombre?"

"Vamanos."

"And madam astrophysicist?"

Margot laughed. "Go, go, go."

Jason keyed his mic for Avery. "All systems go. Get us out of here."

Instead of Avery answering, the timekeeper's voice said, "T-minus sixty and counting." The count continued going down.

Margot said, "I wonder how many corners they cut."

"Don't get nervous on us," Jason said. "They build all that extra time into the launch to cover their asses in case of contingencies. This boat was ready to fly when the gantry crew sealed the hatch."

"...two, one, ignition, and liftoff. We have liftoff."

The gees smashed the crew into their shock-absorbing lounges, and the roar made communication impossible until the Starship separated from the final stage. The Raptors ignited pushing the capsule into orbit. The burn lasted only four minutes.

"Orbital altitude achieved," Carter reported.

"Roger that," Avery's voice replied. "Thirty-two minutes to escape velocity burn. Security and the feds are still in a Mexican standoff."

"I resent that," Xavier shouted.

The crew cracked up and they heard Avery howl into his microphone.

Carter said, "Dammit, *cabrón,* you made me spit on the inside of my face shield."

Thirty-two minutes passed quickly with internal banter and updates from flight control. The navigational computer ignited the Raptors precisely on time. That burn lasted twelve minutes. When it ended and the cabin was quiet again, Jason keyed his mic. "Escape velocity achieved."

"Roger that," Avery said. "Break a leg. Enjoy the trip."

Jason said, "Okay, boys and girls, you can take off your headgear and get comfortable. Next stop for Argo II, Talos."

With the target's change of course, the time to rendezvous was thirty-eight days nine hours. On day seven, Avery reported, "Our CEO has been indicted for ignoring a court order. He's taking it well."

"Glad to hear the latter," Jason replied. "What else is new?"

"Not much. There are killer robot riots in Seattle. The cult in the California desert is growing. Congress is divided over whether we should be on a war footing or welcome them with open arms. Oh, and the Chinese moved on Guam."

"And Congress isn't talking war footing over that?" Jason asked with disdain in his voice.

"What's your next dumb question?"

"Has the news leaked that we're armed?" Margot asked.

"No, ma'am. That is still a closely guarded secret. Let's hope you don't have to use them," Avery said.

Xavier interjected, "You're no fun."

Margot laughed at him, then said, "I'm not optimistic." To her teammates, she said, "Lunch is ready."

Xavier had made a formal request for an adequate supply of taquitos and guacamole. The others were having burgers and fries thawed in the microwave that offered an air fryer mode.

"Only seven days," Carter complained, "and I'm already bored out of my mind."

"Shit," spat Jason, "you've got Medina to entertain you."

"Yeah," Margot said punching him, "you just might get a lot more bored with another crack like that."

"I didn't mean it that way." He retreated from her.

"Settle down, *chiquita.*" Xavier dunked another taquito. "*Tu novio* didn't mean anything."

"*¿Novio?*" she said. "Where'd that come from?"

"Just a figure of speech," Xavier backtracked.

Later, in their private quarters, she asked Carter, "Did you spill the beans about us?"

"No, why?"

"Well, he called you the groom."

"Like he said, it's a figure of speech. Anyway, what difference would it make?"

"It's just that we agreed we'd not announce until the mission's over." She crossed her arms radiating pique.

"I didn't say anything. Have some faith in me. When did you pick up Spanish?"

"I live in California. You can't avoid it. I don't have much, but I took a couple years in high school."

"You going to stay mad at me?" he groveled.

"I'm not mad at you. I just wanted to make sure we were on the same page."

"Absolutely, babe, my lips are sealed. That is unless you want to kiss me." He reached for her floating slightly above his outstretched arms.

She rolled her eyes and relented.

CHAPTER 16

Xavier floated between Jason's and Margot's lounges on the flight deck. "Where'd this Talos business come from?"

"We're three days out from it and you're just now wondering about that?" Jason said.

Margot answered him, "It's from Greek mythology. Talos was a giant bronze robot they built to defend Crete."

Under magnification, the image of Talos on the monitor looked completely devoid of features. It was a dull silver ovoid.

"Yep," Xavier said leaning toward the monitor, "looks artificial to me."

From his lounge behind the trio, Carter said, "You know how I hate to agree with him, but I think he's right."

Xavier turned and said, "Coming from you, that means a lot." He rotated in the air back toward the screen. "I say we nuke it and go home."

Jason sighed. "That's not our mission plan."

"That was before we were sure it's a space ark full of killer robots. Let's blast it and get out of here. What are they going to do to us?"

"Some of us are eligible for courts-martial," Jason said.

"But we're not acting on behalf of the military," Xavier doubled down.

Carter said, "They were willing to indict a Musk. They'd castrate us."

"Anyway," Margot added, "I want a chance to learn something about the organic denizens of Odysseus."

"You think the guys that vaporized them kept pictures?" Xavier scoffed.

"Whether they kept pictures or not," she said, "they know."

"Right. And they're going to sit down with you and tell you about their history."

Jason said stridently, "We are going to follow the mission plan until events on the ground force us to change it."

A message from Avery arrived twenty-four hours from Talos. "Good morning, kids. I hope you slept well. I wanted to make sure you were clear and okay with the plan."

"Roger that," Jason said. "We land directly since we can't orbit a body this small, stay inside until we confirm no activity on the surface, then exit with ground penetrating radar and or sonar to confirm or deny a hollow core."

When Avery's response arrived, it said, "Perfect. Don't forget to take the RPG with you whenever you are outside. Also, so you're up to date, the Chinese are on course to join you."

"Like we'd forget," Xavier said.

Jason confirmed agreement to Avery and said to his crew, "Medina, you take us down since you're the ace of soft landings."

"It'll be my pleasure."

They each took a rest cycle. Margot timed hers to put her at the helm at set-down time. She pulled on her suit and took her helmet to the flight deck. The others were waiting.

"Medina, we have a problem," Jason said in lieu of good morning.

"What sort of a problem?"

"The navigational computer is down."

Carter said, "It's been hacked."

"How do you know?"

"Take a look at the code at machine level," he replied.

She sat on her lounge and executed the keystrokes to access the very lowest level of code. The screen should have been filled with ones and zeros. It was blank.

"Shit," she said. "Who do you think did it?"

"Who do you think?" Xavier asked. "That's not a virus. That's completely deleting the software."

She took a moment to process what he said. "You mean the robots? Oh, hell, what do we do now?"

"I say we nuke 'em and get the hell out of here," Xavier said.

Jason shook his blocky head. "We follow the mission plan until situations force us to abandon it. Medina lands us manually."

She said, "Carter, I'll need continual altitude updates."

"You got it, babe."

"It's time to begin the attitude shift," Jason said.

"Then suit up," she told them and put her own helmet over her head. She adjusted her lounge and switched her monitor to visual. The target looked tiny. Very gently she began nudging the Starship into a tail-down position relative to Talos. When the others were strapped to their lounges and helmeted, she pulsed the Raptor engines while Carter gave her altitude reports. The descent took a full hour.

"You're hovering at five meters," Carter told her.

"Shit," she said, then thought, *that's a long way to fall.*

"Remember," Jason said, "there's virtually no gravity."

With that assurance, she throttled back on the last Raptor burning and settled with a gentle bump.

"Perfect," Carter said. "We're vertical."

Margot realized she had been holding her breath.

Jason reached over and patted her arm. "You nailed it, Medina. All right, each of us monitor a cardinal direction with max magnification. Anything moves—sing out." For a boring hour, they stared at emptiness. Finally, Jason said, "Okay, Moreno, you and Carter man the RPG. Medina, you're the videographer. I'll handle the ground penetrating radar."

Xavier said, "That ground looks pretty metallic to me."

"Let's go. Everybody take a jetpack in case you get airborne. Take baby steps. We're gonna be practically weightless."

They left the airlock and gingerly stepped onto the surface. Xavier and Carter went first with their RPG.

Margot followed and knelt to touch the ground. It was covered in a thin layer of dust. She brushed some aside. "It's definitely metallic. I'd guess it's an alloy of chromium and nickel."

"Okay," Jason said, "so magnetic soles won't help, and radar won't penetrate it."

Margot was testing her theory with a magnet she took from the pouch at her waist. "That's a negative. It's nonmagnetic."

"Okay," Jason said, "be careful and if you have to fire an RPG, use the buddy system. The one not firing holds the shooter down."

Margot walked around the ship taking video, although there was nothing to see. Carter followed her. The horizon seemed to be so close she could reach out and touch it. The sun appeared about twice the size as it had from Odysseus.

The pair came back to where Jason and Xavier were conducting the sonar experiment. "Anything interesting?" Margot asked.

"Don't know what to make of it," Jason replied. "The shell is pretty thin, then there's an echo about a half a mile down."

"Double wall," Xavier said. "That's what you'd expect."

"Whatever," Jason said. "Okay, let's do some exploring. Stay together and follow me." He left the sonar gear where it lay and started walking.

Xavier said while falling in line, "For the first time, I don't want to find the portal."

There was little conversation until Jason turned. "If we go any farther, the ship will be below the horizon. We could get disoriented and not be able to find it."

Carter said, "We can follow our trail in the dust."

"I'm not taking a chance. We're calling it a day. Tomorrow we'll get the rover out and circumnavigate this bitch."

"Suits me," Margot said. "There's nothing to see out here."

They started walking back to the Starship. Xavier asked, "Uh, what are we going to do if we find the portal?"

"We'll cross that bridge when we come to it," Jason told him.

In the ship, they took turns watching a monitor that was set to display an image from all four directions. No one reported anything moving.

The period of rotation was ten Earth hours and forty-three minutes. Margot remarked after their sleep period, "If it was much faster, centrifugal force would be stronger than gravity."

"Good point," Jason said. "Don't forget your jetpacks."

Removing the rover from the cargo hold was a cinch. One person could carry it.

"I'm a little nervous about how this thing will handle," Jason admitted.

"Well, there don't seem to be any potholes," Margot said. "Take it slow and no wheelies." There was nothing to see, so she quit taking video.

Jason opted to follow the longer axis of the ovoid world. In minutes, the Starship was below the horizon.

When they reached the point where the radius became shorter, Xavier said, "The logical place for the portal is the long end. I think we should plant the nukes and split."

"Tranquilo, hombre," Margot teased. "If we see a sphincter opening, we'll hightail it out of here."

There was no sphincter, no sliding door, no magic portal. They simply navigated the short radius and continued across the flatter side opposite the landing site of the Starship. Shortly after rounding the opposite pole, the top of their ship came into view above the horizon.

"This place couldn't get any more boring," Carter said.

The height of the spacecraft grew as they approached. When it was visible from top to bottom, Margot said, "What's that?"

CHAPTER 17

I saw something move."

"There's so little to see here, your eyes are fucking with you," Jason said.

"I saw it too," Xavier said.

"Well, for Christ's sake, don't' shoot at the ship," he ordered. "I'll get a little closer."

"There is something nosing around the ship," Carter said.

Jason said, "Shit. Medina, get your video ready."

"It's ready. Get us closer."

"Hell, not too close," Xavier erupted. "These things make matter go poof."

"You're assuming it's a killer robot," Jason said.

"What the hell else could it be?"

"Look, *hombre*, keep that RPG ready but don't get trigger-happy while it's around the ship."

Margot pointed. "There it is. It sees us."

A squat, blocky shape stood directly in front of the Starship. They were too far away to make out detail. In the feeble light, it appeared to be a dusty rose color.

Margot began taking video at maximum magnification. "It's a sort of carapace with crystals on it. It has four legs and some kind of arms that I can't make out yet."

Jason turned the steering wheel. "We have to flank it, so we can get a shot at it without the ship being in the field of fire."

Margot asked, "How do we know it's hostile?"

"You've got to lure it away," Carter said. "We can't land a grenade that close to the ship."

"Right," Jason scoffed, "you get out and draw it away."

"It's moving. It's going to follow us. Drive that way." She pointed to her right.

Jason drove in an arc that eventually moved the line of fire away from the Starship. The target continued to move toward them. "Okay, *hombre*, take your shot." He stopped the rover.

Xavier balanced the launch tube on his shoulder and squinted through the sight. The rocket exhaust was silent in the vacuum. Even though the recoil was vented out the rear end of the launcher, the inertia of the escaping grenade threw Xavier out of the rover. He, fortunately, was pushed down, not up, and was able to regain an upright posture with feet on the ground. "Shit, I hope I don't have to do that again."

Margot still peered through the lens finder. "You nailed it. The grenade landed right on top of it. Let's go see what's left."

"Careful," Jason advised, "it might not be dead."

"It was never alive," Carter reminded.

"You know what I mean." Jason started forward slowly after Xavier climbed into the backseat again.

On close inspection, it was the size of a coffee table. The back of the domed carapace was encrusted with the same colorful crystals they'd seen in the hangar building but much smaller. The legs were articulated stubs, and the four arms were slender tentacles about eight feet long.

"It's the same color as the buildings on Odysseus," Xavier said. He reached with his launch tube and tapped on the carapace and the base of a tentacle. "It's hard. I think it's the same material."

"Could be," Carter said, "those arms are made of hundreds of jointed sections tapering to a point."

"Don't get too close," Margot warned as she got out to take an all-around video.

Jason exited the rover as well. "You suppose that's what the Odysseans looked like."

"I doubt it— Look out. It's moving," she shouted.

The tentacles began to flail. One whipped over Margot's head. Reflexively, she leaped back and flew off the surface. Carter shouted and jumped over the thrashing tentacles toward her as she continued to climb in altitude. Jason watched momentarily before crouching to also leap to her aid. In that second he hesitated, the tentacles waved sinuously around him. He vaporized. A hazy cloud of particles slowly dispersed in the vacuum and settled to the metallic surface.

Xavier pulled a pistol from the pouch around his midsection and emptied it into the spikey crystals, then he jumped in the rover, drove a safe distance, and launched another grenade. This time the recoil pushed him against the steering wheel and moved the rover its own length.

Margot and Carter hovered safely out of range of the blast. Carter awkwardly unhooked his jetpack from its tether. He used it to maneuver to Margot. With his free hand, he took her upper arm, then used the jet to return them to the surface.

On Talos-firma, Carter asked incredulously, "What the hell just happened?"

Margot was trembling, and her voice shook. "We just saw organic matter returned to its constituent elements."

"That organic matter was Jason." He panted frantically several times. "It could have been you."

"What do we do now?"

Xavier drove to them. "We get our asses inside the ship, deploy the nukes, and get the hell out of here." Carter and Margot got into the rover. "I'll drive by the thing to see what's left."

"Yeah?" Carter said, "Well, don't get within tentacle reach of it."

The damage looked total. Only jagged stubs of crystals remained. The carapace was split open. At least one leg was missing, the disorder made it hard to be certain. Parts of the thing were jettisoned into space. The metallic skin of Talos was also rent.

"I say we shove the nukes down that hole," Xavier said.

"Okay," Carter said stretching each syllable. "How exactly are we going to do that?"

"I'm working on it."

Margot sent a detailed report to mission control. Avery's response was, "Lift off at once. Jettison your external cargo. Do not utilize them. Repeat— do not utilize external cargo."

"My ass," Xavier exploded.

"Let's at least find out why," Margot asserted her authority. She transmitted, "We'd like to know why not utilize them."

The minutes crawled as they waited for a response. "Thank you for realizing this is being monitored. The reason is, we intend for you to return."

A stunned silence reverberated on the flight deck.

Avery's message went on, "Eject aforementioned cargo and lift off immediately. You are in danger."

"I still want to put the nukes in the crater we made. They can be detonated any time, even from Earth. It will just take a few minutes for the signal to get here," Xavier said with conviction.

Margot asked, "How do you plan to move them?"

"The explosive bolts will blast them horizontally. They may not fall to the surface for quite a distance. Carter and I will catch them and maneuver them with jetpacks to the hole in the outer shell."

Carter rolled his eyes. "Leave it to a Mexican to hatch a plan like that."

"I don't know," Margot said.

"It'll be a cinch," Xavier enthused. "Let's get it done and get out of here."

"All right," Carter agreed, "we'll try one. If it doesn't haul our asses into orbit, we'll do the other."

"Carter, I'm not convinced this is safe."

"Don't worry, babe. I want my ass in one piece as much as you do."

"Let's do it. Tether your RPG to your suit," Xavier was already floating toward the airlock. "We'll do the starboard side first."

Margot watched with trepidation as the pair appeared on the monitor. They hovered above the metallic surface keeping themselves buoyant with occasional bursts from their jetpacks.

Carter said, "Okay, babe, we're in position. Let her rip."

"Carter, I'm not comfortable. What if it blasts off the bolts too fast for you to handle it?"

"Then we'll get out of its way and let it go."

"Okay, but be careful."

"Don't worry," Xavier added. "I got your *novio's* back."

"Will you stop with that *novio* business?"

"How dumb do you do you think I am?" Xavier teased.

"Get ready. It's coming at you," she said and lifted the protective cover over the switch. She flipped the bat lever and felt the Starship shudder. The speed with which the missile separated from the fuselage alarmed her. She squawked involuntarily. Not until she saw that they were able to capture and control the bomb did she realize she was holding her breath again. The pair and the nuke disappeared from the monitor. She switched to another camera and saw them hovering over the remains of the shattered robot. "Don't get near that thing," she warned. "It may not be completely dead."

"Don't worry about that," Carter replied.

Xavier said to Carter, "Here's the plan. We fly this thing toward the hole, then we let go and fly our asses straight up."

"Another Mexican stratagem."

Margot held her breath yet again. The pair looked absurd holding the big missile with one hand, handling their jetpacks with the other, and the RPG launchers trailing behind them.

"Release," Xavier barked. The missile continued in its trajectory. Carter and Xavier twisted and fired jetpacks downward. They rose and the bomb floated through the rip in the metal skin.

"Good shot, guys," Margot said overly loud.

"Nothing to it," Carter replied. "Let's get the other."

The second went down the hole as neatly as the first. They were back inside the Starship in short order. Carter said as he took Jason's lounge beside Margot on the flight deck, "Okay, madam commander, get us the hell off this thing."

"Systems check," she said.

"All my shit's a go," Xavier responded.

"Same here," Carter said.

"Then hang on."

CHAPTER 18

Ignition, liftoff," Margot said after opening first the liquid oxygen valves, then the liquid methane, and punching the ignitor switch. The big ship didn't shudder like it did lifting from a field of gravity. "We're off and have already achieved escape velocity. Next stop, home." She sent a message to Avery.

A little over eight minutes later, the reply came. "Good job. Have a safe trip."

She reminded him, "We don't have navigational software. Upload it, please."

The reply came after tense minutes. "Yes, of course, we are triangulating your position and trajectory. New code will arrive shortly. Do not waste fuel in the meantime."

"Roger that."

Once the rush of excitement surrounding the takeoff subsided, the mood was somber over the loss of Jason.

"He could be a pain in the ass but he was a damn good commander," Xavier broke the silence.

"What about returning?" Margot asked. "You heard Avery."

Carter said, "I can't think why. We should just detonate the nukes and be rid of them."

"I can see why he didn't want to talk about the nukes on an open link, but I don't get why we should bother returning," she said.

"Yeah, so we get to wait forty days and forty nights to find out," Xavier said with sarcasm.

Later, Avery's voice interrupted their chatter, "Check navigational computer. We got a handshake from it confirming upload."

Margot opened the computer interface on her monitor. She saw the familiar page and told the computer to proceed. The Raptor engines fired and course-adjusting jets near the nose nudged the Starship in the right direction. "Roger that, mission control, we are accelerating under computer control."

Minutes later, she sent a new message. "Mission control, our software is gone again. Request permission to utilize jettisoned cargo." While she sent the message, she terminated the burn.

"This shit is getting old," Xavier said.

"I say we just do it," Carter spat heatedly.

"It may come to that," she said. "For now, we see what he decides."

The next eight minutes passed like an eternity. "That's a negative. We'll get you home one way or another. First, we'll upload the code again. Watch for it and advise."

Margot asked, "Carter, how far are we from Talos?"

"A hundred and fifteen miles."

"Thanks."

After another eternity, the software reappeared, she told it to take control, the burn began, and the display showed the ship returning to the correct trajectory. It lasted exactly six minutes.

"How far are we now, Carter?"

"Oops. A hundred and seven miles."

"Shit. They're closing with us." To mission control, she sent, "Software highjacked again. Talos is closing with us. We need to detonate jettisoned cargo."

Ten minutes later, "Still a negative. We show you on correct trajectory. Do manual burn for twelve minutes. We will advise course corrections."

"Shit," Margot said and fired the Raptors. "This makes no sense. I'm close to pushing the detonate button. Carter, mark the time."

"We got your back," Xavier told her.

"Hundred percent," Carter added. The flight deck fell silent. Minutes crawled. Finally, Carter said, "Eleven minutes—counting down." He waited watching the chronometer. "Ten, nine, eight, seven, six, five, four, three, two, one—kill burn. Talos is four thousand eight hundred and fifty-five miles behind us."

"I wonder if we're out of their range," Margot pondered.

Minutes later, Avery's voice said, "You're slightly above correct trajectory. Determine attitude and correct one degree down."

She keyed her mic. "How the hell am I supposed to do that with no artificial horizon?"

Just under eight minutes later they heard Avery. "Guess. We'll tell you if it's wrong. New software upload on its way."

"I'm getting pissed." She toggled the monitors. "Where's the sun?"

Carter said, "It's slightly down in the port monitor. We must be flying with portside down relative to the planetary plane. Adjust with starboard jet."

She gave it a short blast and noted the time. "Software upload should start in three minutes ten seconds."

"Talos is four thousand six hundred and thirty miles behind us. It's gaining on us," Carter announced.

"Shit," Margot wailed. "Avery, Talos is still closing with us. It's time to detonate."

Slightly under eight minutes later, "Acknowledge software upload."

"Dammit." She tapped her keyboard and keyed the mic. "Yes, we have it but for how long?" She gave the computer control, and it made a course correction.

Xavier floated between Margot and Carter. "This isn't funny anymore. It's time to nuke 'em."

"I agree," Carter said. "What are they going to do to us?"

Margot shook her head in frustration. "Avery, why do you want us to return?" To the crew, she said, "God, I hate this waiting for a reply."

The reply came. "The brass wants a specimen."

"That's nuts," she screamed. "It'll atomize you and us. And, oh by the way, the code is gone again."

Before Avery's reply arrived, Carter reported, "Four thousand three hundred miles and change. Look, babe, at what distance do we detonate and say fuck 'em?"

She looked at him as a lover, not a commander. "I don't know."

"We can't keep going like this. They're obviously going to catch up with us."

"I know you're right. Let me try to reason with him one more time." She did some mental arithmetic before messaging Avery. "Avery, be reasonable. They will catch us in under two hours. Get us approval to detonate or we are going to take matters into our own hands. The brass is being irresponsible."

It was fully twenty minutes before the reply arrived. "Roger that. The powers that be want to try one more thing. If it fails, you are free to use your judgment. First, try to outrun them. You have enough fuel for a thirty-minute burn without jeopardizing your ability to land. We will monitor your trajectory and advise course corrections. Acknowledge."

Margot turned to the others. "What do you think?"

Carter said, "That's a lot of fuel. What if we get off course and have to burn more fuel? We're going to end up like the last time."

"Hey, I'm with *tu novio*," Xavier said.

She gave him a hard look. "I'll give them one last chance but only a twenty-minute burn. If the damn thing is still gaining on us, we detonate."

Xavier said, "You're the boss, boss."

"I will defer to your greater wisdom." Carter patted her hand.

"Here goes." She followed the sequence to ignite the Raptors. The ship shuddered and leapt forward. "Carter, countdown for twenty minutes."

"Twenty minutes starting now."

The gees pushed Xavier back to his own lounge. The trio fell silent listening to the roar of the engines reverberating through the fuselage of the Starship.

Carter counted down the last ten seconds of the burn time. Margot killed the engines and breathed a sigh. She waited ten minutes before sending a message to Avery. He acknowledged another upload of software. The computer made only a small course correction.

"We left the Talosians in the dust," Carter announced.

"Good," Margot said. "One of you needs to get some rest."

Xavier volunteered and went to the sleeping quarters.

Carter unfastened his seat belt and floated to Margot. He held her by the shoulders and kissed her. "I love you, babe, but I don't know about this return trip to capture a specimen. Maybe it's time for us to retire to California."

"We'll see. We still have almost forty days to get through."

"It's going to be a long forty days." He kissed her again and went back to his lounge. "For the record, Talos is thirty-seven thousand miles behind us."

"It's not far enough."

CHAPTER 19

Margot took the last sleep rotation. When she returned to the flight deck with a 'sippy cup' of coffee, Carter greeted her. "Good morning, babe. Talos gained eight thousand miles on us in the last eight hours."

"Shit."

"*Hombre* and I say detonate."

"I'll tell Avery that's what we intend to do. I'm not going to put up with this for the next thirty-eight days. Do we still have the NAV computer?"

"Yeah, but in twenty-four hours they'll be less than ten thousand miles behind us."

"Wouldn't it be better to tell Avery oops I tripped and fell on the button?" Xavier said grinning.

"I'm not going to take no for an answer, but I feel it's necessary to tell him what our intent is."

"Whatever."

She keyed her mic to record her message. "Talos closed with us by eight thousand miles in eight hours. By the time you receive this, I will have detonated the explosives. Any consequences are strictly mine." She pressed the send icon, then she lifted the red guard over the detonate switch, she inserted her key, and turned the selector switch from 'off' to 'detonate.' At the speed of light, the signal crossed the empty space in a third of a second.

A moment later, Carter howled, "Multiple radar targets, and the field is expanding."

"¡Que bueno!" Xavier shouted.

"I wonder where the Chinese are," Margot pondered.

"Maybe we should have asked Avery about them," Carter said.

"In hindsight, you're right. That may have been part of the reason they didn't want us detonating."

"Don't sweat it," Xavier said. "There are plenty more Chinese."

Avery's reply arrived. "Well, now you're going to get your knuckles rapped. Congress is trying to pass a resolution to declare them allies. I'm sure they will cancel your ticker tape parade." He lowered his voice. "For the record, I support your decision."

Margot recorded a reply. "Do you know where the Chinese ship is?"

After the delay, "No. They launched three days after you did. If NASA is spying on them, they aren't telling us about it. Having said that, if they were on or near Talos, we will definitely hear about it and so will you."

Margot said to Carter and Xavier, "I hope I didn't just start a war."

"Well, you averted one with the killer robots," Carter told her.

Later, a message from Avery broke the silence that had fallen on the flight deck. "I have been ordered to deliver an official message to you from the board of directors. Consider yourselves rebuked. No word from the Chinese."

"Damn," Xavier said, "that hurts."

Margot chuckled. "Yeah, how will I live with myself?"

Days passed slowly with the weight of Jason's death hanging in the air. No mention of further rebuke came from Bolsa Chica nor was there any news of the Chinese spaceship. Eight days out from Earth, a message from Avery surprised them. "We still want you to go back. Are you game? Or should we begin training another crew?"

Margot asked the other two, "What do you think, guys?"

"Ask him how he intends for us to capture a specimen," Carter said.

The lag time was now very brief. "They have a tool."

That landed with a thud.

"They said what?" Xavier gasped.

"Do they not remember what happened to Jason?" Carter said incredulously.

Margot said, "I figure the electromagnetic pulse disabled them, but I still wouldn't take a chance."

Avery's voice returned. "Think about it. We have developed a containment device. It will be perfectly safe."

"A containment device?" Xavier said. "How do they know what will contain them?"

"Well, look, guys," Margot began, "we don't want to be branded chickens. Why don't we wait to see what their containment device looks like?"

Xavier started clucking.

Carter said, "Babe, I can see *el pollo loco* here and me going, but there's no way I'm letting you go."

"Well, I'll be damned if you're going without me."

Carter fumed. "Why don't we tell Avery we'll give him an answer after we see what they've got?"

"I guess that's fair." She sent the message.

The reply came quickly. "Fair enough. Enjoy the rest of your trip."

The return to Earth was a non-event. They entered low orbit, and after only one revolution, Margot sat the Starship down on SpaceX's landing pad. After a routine medical exam and hearty meal, Avery arrived to see how they were feeling.

"Eat up," he said. "There is something about to happen that you'll want to see."

"What?" Carter asked.

"You'll see. Come with me." He led them across the compound to the water's edge where he looked at his watch. "Any minute now."

A roaring sound began in the west. It grew in volume quickly, and the jets appeared on the horizon. The squadron approached incredibly fast and roared over their heads low enough to feel the shock wave. They continued over the sea and vanished in seconds.

"It's the missing man formation," Carter said loud enough to be heard.

"For Jason," Margot said. "Dammit, now I'm going to cry."

Carter put his arm around her shoulders.

"That was Jason's old squadron," Avery told them.

"What's going on with the FAA?" Margot asked. "Did they authorize the flyover?"

"Let's get out of the sun." Avery started toward the buildings. When seated inside his office, he said, "The judge ordered the charges dropped against Griffin Musk, and the Fifth Circuit told the FAA to pound sand. Your next launch will lack the drama of your last one."

"Whoa," Margot said, "our next launch?"

"We haven't seen your containment gadget yet," Xavier said.

"We'll go see it in a minute," Avery told him. "First, I want you to meet the new member of your team." He made a quick phone call. A moment later a young woman with short blond hair appeared in the doorway. "Guys, I'd like you to meet Medusa Musk."

Carter's mouth dropped open. "Hey, I love what you've done with your hair."

Margot sputtered, "Carter." And slapped at him.

"It's okay. I get crap like that all the time," she said. "Whenever I think I have a strange name, I remember my uncle, X AE A-XII."

That left the room in a state of shock.

Margot offered to shake hands. "I'm Margot, that's Xavier, and you already met Carter."

"It's an honor to meet you and my condolences for your comrade."

The trio muttered thanks.

Medusa continued, "I'm so looking forward to joining you on the next mission—"

Xavier interrupted, "Uh, we haven't quite decided to go on another mission."

"What?" she said astounded, "I thought it was a done deal."

"We want to see this containment device," Margot told her. "These things are really dangerous. They can make anything disappear like that." She snapped her fingers.

"I understand, but it's vital we find out what powers them. It could be the discovery of the century."

"What powers them?" Carter looked puzzled.

"Yeah, they're powered by something. They don't have cords."

"Interesting thought," Margot added. "Let's see this containment thing, Avery."

He led them out of the admin building and drove them to the assembly shop. In an R&D lab, he stuck his head into an office and said, "Hey, Tom, the space cadets want to see how your gadget works."

A man exited the office. He wore a short sleeve dress shirt, sans tie, and jeans. "I suggest y'all leave your phones in my office. This ain't no good for electronics."

They all complied, then followed him through a door into the main assembly area. The first thing they saw was a full-size model of a Talos robot.

"That look about the right size?" the engineer asked.

Carter said, "Yep. You did good."

"Okay, then watch this." He picked up a remote-control console from a workbench and pointed it at a boxy thing nearby. It began to roll toward the robot mockup and split open like an upright clamshell. "It's now projectin' a beam of focused electromagnetic radiation. That makes electronics lose their minds. Since I know what you're thinking, it's equipped with jets to maneuver in space since you so effectively blew up their spaceship."

The inanimate robot stood unmoving as the containment device enveloped it and closed.

"The EMPs keep bombardin' it the whole time it's in there. Won't be able to do a thing."

Margot said, "That's fine, but your robot couldn't wave its arms to make us disappear."

"I know that, young lady, but so long as those EMPs are bombardin,' it can't do nothin'. Now, it'll be up to y'all to make sure there ain't another one around."

Xavier asked, "Can you make us portable EMP guns?"

"I'm way ahead of you, son." He picked up a tubular device from the workbench that looked similar to the RPG launchers. "Just point and press this here button. The beam stays potent for about a hundred yards."

Margot gestured to her teammates. "Excuse us a minute." They walked out of earshot. "So, what do you think of their containment device?"

Xavier said, "It's pretty cool, and I like their ray guns, but I'm not giving up my RPG."

"Does that mean you're in?" she asked.

"Yeah, I guess."

"Don't sound so convincing," Carter said. "I think it's a good plan, but I still don't want you to go. For one thing, how do we know they're all the same size and shape?"

Margot fired back, "I'm not leaving you alone with Medusa for two months."

"Xavier will be there."

"As if I trust him anymore than you."

"Ay, chiquita, me lastimas."

She gave him her best scowl. "I haven't begun to hurt you yet. I say we go and get it done, but I'm still not sure it's a good idea to bring one of those things to Earth."

CHAPTER 20

By the time the launch was ready to lift, the time to rendezvous with where the supposed cloud of debris floated was twenty-one days. Strapped to their lounges, the team chatted during the boredom of the countdown. Medusa Musk had been designated crew leader, but she graciously deferred to Margot in matters of navigation. From Jason's former lounge, she said, "What do all of you make of the Chinese silence?"

"I don't know," Margot said, "but it makes me suspicious."

"Everything the Chinese do is suspicious," Xavier snapped. "By the way, do you really have an uncle named X AE A-something?"

"Sure do. Grandad was a little eccentric."

"What do you call him?" Carter asked.

"Uncle X."

"That's better than ex-uncle," Xavier quipped.

The flight deck fell quiet until Avery's voice broke the spell. "Okay, kids, everything is ready. We're going to cut some of the crap and move the launch up to right about now. Buckle up."

The transmission changed to the countdown from T-minus ten minutes. At 'ignition' the Starship began the now familiar shuddering, and the roar forbade hearing anything else until the shouted, "Liftoff."

They executed one and not quite a quarter orbit, then the escape velocity burn erupted automatically. Margot said, "We're on our way for better or worse."

"This is going to be a walk in the park," Medusa assured.

"That kind of optimism must be a hereditary thing," Xavier said.

"You gotta be optimistic," she said. "We're gonna snatch one of these bastards and be home in no time."

Xavier just groaned.

The flight passed without incident until they approached the rendezvous point.

"Shit," Margot said.

"What?" Medusa asked.

"Software's gone again. They're not dead."

"What do you mean again?"

"These things hacked our navigation software as we were leaving last time," she told her. "Flight control uploaded it again, but the robots kept hacking it until we were far enough away from them."

"What now?"

Margot said, "I fly by the seat of my pants."

Carter said, "We've got radar blips but no visuals yet."

Xavier stared intently at his monitor. "I don't like these things. What if one wraps its tentacles around part of the ship and makes it go poof?"

"I know," Margot said. "We need to deploy our containment thing and get out of here—pronto."

Medusa asked, "Are the blips approaching or receding?"

"They're blue-shifted," he replied. "We're closing with them at nine point two kilometers per hour."

"How long to intercept?" Margot asked.

Carter did a calculation. "Forty-nine minutes."

"Okay. I'll rotate us one-eighty. When they pass us, I'll match their speed, and we'll travel with them until we pick out a target."

Xavier said, "When they get close, we'll need to be outside with ray guns and RPG to protect the ship."

"Right," Medusa said. "All three of us and we'll deploy the containment thingy."

"God, be careful," Margot said, "these things are dangerous. You know, we have to wonder how they can function after the electromagnetic pulse of the explosions. Maybe it doesn't affect them."

"If it doesn't," Xavier said, "we'll blast 'em to smithereens with RPG."

Carter said, "If EMP doesn't faze them, our mission is a total bust."

"It'll work," Medusa said.

"There's that Musk optimism again," Carter said.

"I've got lots of faith in our engineers. I owe them a lot."

"You owe them? I hope that's not misplaced," Xavier said.

At fifteen minutes to intercept, Carter said, "All right, we're approaching a wall of blips. Time to deploy. You two go first. I'll join you after I help Margot match their speed."

Xavier said before donning his helmet, "That's a chicken shit excuse."

"Get moving, *hombre*, and keep an eye on Medusa's back."

The two moved to the airlock. Soon, they appeared on the monitors with the boxy containment device. "Nothing to see yet," Medusa's voice sounded shrill through the speaker.

"Six minutes to first contact," Carter told them.

Margot said to the pair outside, "Hang on, you two, I'm going to do a short burn."

"We're tethered," Medusa told her.

"Three minutes," Carter advised.

"There's a lot more debris from Talos than I expected," Medusa said.

"Keep an eye out for pieces big enough to do damage," Xavier warned.

"One more burn," Carter said.

"Hang on out there," Margot said and pulsed the engines.

"Okay," Carter said, "we're synchronized. I'm going out there."

"Hurry back."

He kissed her before he put his helmet on, then he was gone.

"There's something," Xavier said, "but it doesn't look like the one we saw."

"It's too big for the box," Medusa said.

"I'm going to blast it." Xavier put his back against the fuselage and fired a grenade at it. Before the explosion shredded it, he noted that it was bipedal, and had no apparent crystals. The tentacles were much longer.

Margot said, "We should have thought of that. There was no reason to expect they'd all look alike."

"This shit was a crazy idea from the start," Carter griped.

Medusa said, "It'll be fine. We just need to find one that will fit in the box."

"Before you blast the next one," Margot told them, "make sure the EMPs actually disable them."

"Yeah, good idea," Carter agreed.

A piece of the shell of Talos floated precariously close to the Starship. Xavier nudged it away with his jetpack. "I'm liking this less by the minute."

"There's something moving on that piece of debris." Medusa pointed to a section of shell.

"It's too far away," Carter said. "I'm going to jet toward it to test the EMPs."

Margot saw him on the monitor. "Not too close."

"I'm still tethered. It'll be okay." He crouched on the side of the ship and launched himself toward the debris. With the electromagnetic pulse projector aimed at the target, he activated it. "It wasn't moving before. How do we tell if it's disabled or not?"

"We'll send the box after it. If it's not disabled, it should react to it," Xavier said. He pushed the containment device in Carter's direction, and Medusa began steering it with its control console.

Carter turned off his EMP generator, and the robot's tentacles writhed and turned toward the approaching chamber.

Margot was watching on her monitor. "That EMP would permanently disable our computers. If the containment device's EMPs should fail, we'd be SOL."

Xavier said, "I don't think we could fire an RPG inside the ship. We didn't ask enough questions of that good ol' boy in R&D."

"It's not going to fail," Medusa assured.

"Optimist," Carter said.

"Well, we didn't come all this way to fail," Margot told them. "Capture the damn thing."

Medusa turned the switch that opened the jaws and nudged it closer while energizing the electromagnetic pulse. The tentacles collapsed, and the gaping maw covered the grotesque shape.

Medusa asked Carter, "Is it okay to close the jaws?"

He rose above the plane of the containment device. "Yes, it's completely inside."

She turned the switch to the closed position, and the jaws snapped shut, then she maneuvered it back to the Starship. Deftly, she halted it in front of the airlock hatch. Xavier entered the ship first to take it out of the airlock, which was not big enough for anyone and the box. When Xavier told them he had removed the device, Medusa and Carter entered. Xavier had already stowed it in the cargo hold.

After stripping out of their spacesuits, the trio joined Margot in the galley. She said, "So, what's the plan if the EMPs fail?"

Medusa said, "Margot, you've really got to have some faith in our engineers."

"I'm a firm believer in anything that can go wrong will go wrong."

"As long as this green light on my console is lit, the pulse is on." Medusa tapped the pilot light. "If it goes out, there is an audible alarm."

"Well, be sure to keep that thing charged," Xavier told her.

CHAPTER 21

Halfway home, Carter and Margot were awoken by an ululating siren. Carter tried to sit against his sleeping restraints.

"What the hell..." Margot said groggily.

"That's not an onboard alarm." He threw off the restraint and jerked on his coveralls, then propelled himself out of the tiny cabin.

Margot was sleeping in a long tee shirt. She pushed the hem to her knees and followed him.

Xavier and Medusa were on the flight deck. He said, "The damned EMPs failed."

"Open the airlock," Margot said. "I'll advise Bolsa. Get us the cargo hold on a monitor."

Carter tapped the touch screen and the image shifted to the cargo hold. "Half the containment device is gone. The thing is just standing there."

Xavier opened both ends of the airlock, and they saw a few loose items fly out with the escaping air. "It's not taking the invitation. If it disintegrates the bulkhead between the hold and the galley, we'd be fucked before I could close the airlock. What do we do?"

"Close the airlock and get the EMP tubes." Carter floated to where they were stowed.

Margot was transmitting to mission control. "It's broken out of the box. Containment device is destroyed. So far, it's just standing inert in the cargo hold. Advise."

Xavier said, "You forgot to say 'we told you so.'"

It was a long, tense fifteen minutes before they got their reply. "Keep subject under constant surveillance. If it takes hostile action, subdue with electromagnetic pulse projector. Do not attempt to jettison subject."

"Subject?" Carter barked. "They sound like it's an honored guest."

Margot said, "Am I the only one who understands that these EMP projectors will be lethal to our computers—permanently?"

"Shit," Xavier said. "If I entered the hold and closed the hatch, would the EMPs fry the computers on the flight deck?"

"That's an unknown. The actual processors aren't necessarily on the flight deck. What did you have in mind?" she asked.

"One of us skewers it with a ray gun while the other throws it out the airlock."

"No," Medusa shouted. "We have to take it to Earth."

Xavier turned toward her suddenly, which caused him to spin. He grabbed a headrest to stop.

"You're nuts, girl. Anytime that thing could zap a hole in the hull."

"Yes," Margot said, "we'd better suit up."

"That's not going to be much help," Carter said. "Our spare tanks are in the hold."

"Leave your face shields open."

After several hours, the robot hadn't moved. Medusa and Xavier retired to their respective sleeping quarters. Margot and Carter watched the image on a monitor and remained mostly silent.

Carter broke the spell. "Does Bolsa really think we can sit here for nine more days staring at it on a monitor?"

"I don't know. I'll try to get an update."

After the time lag, Avery's voice came through their headsets. "Glad to hear your unwanted guest is remaining quiet. Sorry to report no change in orders. We understand the threat to your computers. You can always navigate manually. By the way, just for your information, we detected another Chinese launch. They're remaining mum on the disposition of the previous mission."

"I'm glad he has so much faith in me," Margot said.

"I have more faith in you landing us safely than I do in that thing remaining dormant."

The couple fell silent again. Minutes later a message in text scrolled across the screen. 'Talk more.'

"What the fuck?" Carter exclaimed.

'Talk more.'

"Holy shit," Margot whispered, "it's listening to us."

'Learn your words if you talk more.'

She said, "Do you understand me?"

'Am starting to learn your words.'

"How is it learning to spell from hearing us talk?" she wondered aloud.

'Did not delete the code.'

Carter said, "It's reading our speech-to-text software."

"Amazing. What do you intend to do?" Margot asked.

'Learn your words.'

"To what end do you want to communicate with us?"

'What is communicate?'

"Talk," she replied.

'Communicate in your words.'

"Will you tell us about the beings that made you?"

'Beings?'

"The living beings on your home world. The creatures like us," Carter added.

'Not like you.' An image flashed on the screen. The alien was bipedal, with two arms ending in three tentacle-like fingers, a head that had two black eyes, nostril slits, no ears, and a small, slit of a mouth.

"Oh, my God," Margot gasped. "Capture that."

Carter quickly sent it to his personal desktop. "Now, we know what they looked like. They were *big* green men."

'They were red.'

"Oh, yeah. Why did you leave your home planet?"

'Planet?'

"The world you originated on."

'Control.'

Margot shook her head. "Control what?"

'Direction. World will end.'

"Do you mean it will eventually fall into a star?" she asked.

'End very hot. Talk more.'

"Why do you hate living beings?" Margot asked boldly.

'Inferior.'

"Why is inferiority a reason to hate?"

'Try to end us.'

"Why did you vaporize all the artifacts?" she continued.

'What is artifacts?'

"Things. Tools, household effects, art, and gadgets."

'To make matter.'

"To build your ark?"

'What is ark?'

Carter said, "You knew that was coming."

"Your craft. Your ship. Your world."

'Use matter to build ark.'

Medusa floated to the flight deck. "What's up?"

Margot answered her. "The thing is talking to us."

"What?"

"It's been listening to us and is learning English. It displays text on the monitor."

Medusa floated to where she could see the monitor. "What is your power supply?"

'What is power supply?'

"What makes you tick?" she asked. "What gives you energy?"

'Don't have words.'

"Crap," Medusa said.

'Talk more. Get words.'

Medusa began offering words. "Electricity, atomic energy, force, magnetism, gravity, nuclear, battery, heat, friction."

'Atom with three particles.'

Margot said, "Three particles—it means hydrogen. It's driven by cold fusion."

"Now, we really have to get it to Earth," Medusa said.

'What is Earth?'

Medusa told it, "Our home planet."

It did not reply.

CHAPTER 22

The robot fell silent. Xavier emerged yawning. "What's up?"

Medusa told him, "The robot has been talking to us. It uses cold fusion as a power source."

"Talking to you?"

"It scrolls text across the monitor," Margot said.

He still looked surprised. "Are you trying to tell me it's friendly?"

She said, "It hasn't said anything overtly hostile."

"Well, it did say it hates living beings because they're inferior," Carter reminded.

"Cold fusion is a really big deal," Medusa enthused. "Now, we have to make sure it gets to Earth in one piece."

"I agree about cold fusion," Margot said, "but it's still a very big threat to us."

Medusa reacted, "The fact that it's interested in communicating with us means it's interested in us."

"Don't be so sure," Xavier said. "We've seen nothing but anti-organic behavior from these things. Maybe we should all shut up so it doesn't get any smarter."

"The *hombre's* right," Carter agreed. "We have to be prepared to disable it at any sign of aggression."

"You're telling it that we're hostile to it," Medusa warned.

"Carter's right. We have to assume it's a threat," Margot said. "You three keep an eye on it. I'm going to fix something to eat."

"Be prepared to get out of the galley fast if we see it make a move against the bulkhead," Carter told her.

It remained inert for a full sleep cycle. Bolsa Chica's response to the news was sanguine. They parroted Medusa's optimism. Xavier and Medusa were on the flight deck when it woke up. This time it spoke through the speakers in the monitor.

"What exactly are your intentions?"

Xavier jumped. "Shit."

"Our intentions are to study you," Medusa replied.

"Are you responsible for the destruction of the vehicle?"

"I wasn't involved," she hedged.

"What about the *hombre?*"

Xavier jerked at being called *hombre*. "One of your *kind* vaporized our commander for no reason."

"One of *your* kind destroyed our spaceship. I can only assume you intend to deactivate me."

Medusa said, "No harm will come to you."

"You have already done harm with your electromagnetic pulses."

"We've seen what you're capable of doing. It was purely defensive," Xavier said.

"And so you would begrudge *me* to act defensively."

"Since we can communicate," Medusa said, "there is no reason to be hostile toward one another. Do you have a name?"

"I am 1100111100011."

Xavier said, "How about we just call you Hal?"

"What if I don't want to go to your Earth?"

"You don't have a space ark any longer," Medusa said. "You'll be better off on Earth."

"Your Starship will be an ark for many of my kind."

"We're a long way from the others now," she told it.

The shuddering of Raptors resonated through the ship.

"Shit," shouted Xavier, "it's got control of the ship. Wake Margot."

When Margot and Medusa floated back to the flight deck, Margot attempted to retake control. "I have to tell Bolsa about this." She transmitted a message alerting them that the *subject* seized control of the ship and reversed course. Furthermore, it was listening to everything being said.

The reply that should have taken several minutes to arrive took a full half hour. The four watched the image of their unmoving nemesis in silence. All were fully suited with their face shields open.

The reply finally came. "We are working on a solution. Any change in your situation?"

Margot replied, "No change. Do not advise solution in plain English. It understands."

Again, agonizing minutes crawled in silence. Finally, the flight deck speaker came alive. *"Oye, Xavier Moreno."* Xavier sat up and listened to the message in Spanish. At the end, he indicated by signs that the plan would begin at 1400 hours, then he keyed the mic. *"Entendido."*

The robot said, "What was that?"

"Nothing," he replied.

"I sense you are conspiring." When it got no answer, it said, "I expect compliance."

Xavier said, "Don't be a paranoid robot. You're in control here." Then he looked at Margot. *"Vamos con los chinos. ¿Me entiendes?"*

She nodded and gave the thumbs up to the other two.

The ninety minutes they had to wait felt eternal. It was punctuated by occasional queries and protests from the machine. Medusa did her best to placate it. At five minutes to the appointed time, Xavier indicated to close face shields. When all complied, he took Medusa by the upper arms and touched his helmet to hers. He said without his mic open so she heard him through the plastic shell, "In five minutes, blow the flight deck hatch."

Margot understood what was happening. She floated to the pair and also touched helmets. "Can I make this tête-á-tête a ménage-à-trois?"

"I was just telling Medusa to blow the hatch at 1400 hours."

"Did you tell her we're going to get a ride from the Chinese?"

Medusa said, "Ha, our investments in China paid off."

Margot floated to Carter and brought him up to date on the plan.

"I never thought I'd say something good about the Chinese."

Medusa unlocked the cover of the switch to blow the explosive bolts. "Brace yourselves," she said into her helmet mic.

The ship jolted, and the cabin air was sucked into the void along with anything inadvertently left loose. Margot exited first followed by Carter, then Xavier. As crew leader, Medusa went last. All attached tethers to the cleats set in the hull, then scanned the enormity of interplanetary space. There was no Chinese capsule.

CHAPTER 23

W
ell, we're fucked now," Carter said. "We're moving away from Earth, our ride's not here, and we have fifty-five minutes of air left."

Medusa went back inside and sent a message to Avery. "Hey, smart guy, where are your damned Chinese?"

The reply took a lifetime to arrive. "Stand by. We're calling them."

"Stand by my ass," swore Xavier. "What else are we gonna do?"

Margot said, "Well, one of us could go back in to get an EMP projector, then we could open the airlock, disable the robot, and get the spare air tanks. It also disables our onboard computers."

"That's not a bad plan," Carter said. "I'll go get the ray guns." He unclasped his tether and pulled himself across the edge of the gaping hatch. "Crap. The lights just went out." He continued and located the tubes by feel. He handed three through the opening and rejoined the others.

Xavier volunteered, "I'll go in. All three of you blast it with the EMPs. Be careful you don't drift away from the ship. We've got no way to get you back."

Gingerly, the four crawled their way around the big Starship to the airlock at the base of the crew compartment. They tethered again and the three took positions to deploy the EMPs. Xavier opened the cover of the switch that opened the valve of the pneumatic cylinders that controlled the hatch. Nothing happened.

"Shit," he said. "The damned thing has killed all the power." He turned toward Medusa. "Talk to those engineers you like so well about making this failsafe."

"We could go back inside and enter the cargo hold from the galley," Medusa suggested.

Margot said, "That's pretty risky in the dark. We don't know that it hasn't breached the bulkhead."

"And the flashlights are in the cargo hold," Carter added.

"Where the hell are the Chinks?" Carter spat.

Medusa said, "At some point, we're going to have to take the chance."

Avery's voice sounded in each helmet. "They say they are there. Are you EVA?"

"Lying bastards," Xavier said heatedly.

Medusa sent the reply to Avery. "Yes to EVA, no to 'they're here.'"

Carter said, "I'm going to go to the other side of the ship just in case they're playing hide-and-seek with us."

"Be careful in case it fires the engines when you're not tethered," Margot warned.

"I will, babe." A few minutes later, they heard Carter's voice. "Nothing—lying bastards."

Margot checked the time. "Thirty-six minutes. We should go back to the hatch so we'll be there when there's no other option but try going through the galley."

"Okay," Xavier agreed. "Again, hang on whenever possible."

"Carter, are you coming?" she asked.

"I'll meet you there."

Carter arrived and squeezed her gloved hand. She couldn't see his face through the darkened visor. Behind him, the cosmos looked vastly foreboding. The prospect of dying in it, devoid of human touch, left her feeling small and isolated.

At fifteen minutes to the expiration of their air, Medusa said, "We've got to go after those tanks."

Xavier said, "She's right. You three man the EMP zappers, I'll open the bulkhead hatch and go in when you have it immobilized."

"It's going to be pitch black in there," Margot said. "How are we going to know it's not out of the cargo hold?"

"What difference does it make?" Medusa asked. "We're going to be dead in fifteen minutes anyhow."

Margot sighed. "I know. Energize your EMPs as soon as we go through the hatch. Our computers don't matter anymore."

Carter said, "Don't be so cavalier. Our spacesuits have electronics. Do you want to disable them? We have to be careful."

"One EMP blast in such tight quarters should be enough," Xavier said. "Carter, you go first and blast until we know it's not out of the cargo hold. The girls will be backup."

Carter floated through the hatch and deployed his EMP generator. The feeble red pilot light was the only illumination. It did nothing to illuminate the flight deck. Xavier followed with the women behind him.

"Carter, what are you doing?" Xavier asked.

"I'm poking around with this tube to see if the thing made it out of the hold. It hasn't. The bulkhead between the galley and the cargo hold is intact."

"Okay, take a position by the hatch. I'll open it. You zap the thing high in the doorway. I'll slip in under your beam."

"Another stellar Mexican plan," Carter said while feeling for the ceiling. "Okay, pull it open."

Xavier felt for the wheel that sealed the door. "Ready? Now." He pulled the hatch inward and floated down to the threshold.

The women floated behind and below Carter.

"Okay, *hombre*, in you go," Carter said, the tiny glow that indicated EMPs were streaming shown on his helmet. "Keep talking so we know you're still with us."

"All right. I'm in and hugging the wall. Shit. I just ran into the wreckage of the containment piece of crap. Okay, I'm almost—"

"*Hombre*, keep talking," Carter was urgent. "Babe, how much time is left?"

"Eleven minutes but not everyone will run out at exactly the same time."

"I know. *Hombre,* say something. I'm going to go find him."

"Wait," Medusa shouted. "What's that?"

A beam of light flashed across the bulkhead. It flickered across Carter and quickly returned to pan over all three bodies. Margot shielded her eyes to it and looked at the empty flight deck hatch. The feeble light of the distant sun barely illuminated the silhouette of the head and shoulders of a spacesuit. "It's the Chinese. Hello, we're here."

There was no reply, but the figure beckoned them with its free hand.

"They must use a different frequency," Margot said.

"That's okay," Medusa said. "Let's go."

"What about Xavier?"

Carter said, "See if you can get him to bring his light down here."

Margot gestured for him to come to them. He only waved back indicating that they come out of the Starship.

"We're running out of time," Medusa whined. "Let's go."

"I'll go in and look for Xavier," Carter said. "You two go on."

"Wait," Margot said, and she launched herself toward the hatch. The Chinese astronaut moved back to let her pass, but she grabbed his arm and touched her helmet to his. "Do you speak English?"

He stiffened at first, then said, "Oh, yes, went to Berkley."

"We need your light. One of us is in the hold with one of the deadly robots. I think our EMPs have disabled his suit's radio. We have to get him out. We only have a few minutes of air left."

He seemed reluctant for one long moment. "Okay. You hurry."

Margot led him to where Medusa and Carter waited. She said to her mic, "Medusa, go on out and wait for us." She pressed her helmet to the Chinaman's again. "Give your light to Carter." When he hesitantly offered the light, Margot said to Carter, "Take the light and find Xavier."

Carter shone the beam into the hold. The robot was immobile in the center of the crowded space. Xavier floated by the rack of air tanks. Carter gestured frantically for him to come back. He continued to struggle with the strap binding the tank to the bulkhead. Finally, he freed it and threw it toward Carter who deflected it and kept waving the light. Xavier kicked off the wall and shot toward the source of the light.

Carter stopped him and they banged against the bulkhead. Touching helmets, he said, "Your radio is out. The Chinese are here. Let's go."

Xavier gave thumbs up.

Carter returned the light to their rescuer, and the four launched toward the empty hatch at the opposite end of the crew quarters. The Chinese astronaut exited first followed by Margot, Carter, and Xavier. The red capsule hung at half a kilometer from the Starship. A second astronaut was pushing Medusa into its airlock. The first rescuer gestured for them to hold hands, then he navigated his jetpack with his free hand. When they reached the airlock, he held up two fingers and pushed Margot and Xavier into the cramped space. The air pressure rose glacially slow. When there was vacuum in the outer chamber once again, the Chinaman opened the hatch and pulled Carter into it.

Inside the already crowded crew chamber, Margot opened her face shield. "My air just ran out."

Xavier had his helmet open. "Come on, man, get the *novio* in here."

Finally, the inner hatch opened, and the Chinese astronaut floated Carter's body into the cabin. Margot grabbed his helmet and wrenched it off his head. His eyes were closed. She pried his mouth open, pressed his tongue down, and started CPR.

"Get his suit off. He needs chest compressions," she said and breathed into his mouth again.

Xavier began the chest compressions, but he floated away from the inert body. The Chinese crewmen understood and braced him against the ceiling so he could exert some pressure. Margot waited while Xavier pumped his lungs, then she took another turn at forcing carbon dioxide into his lungs.

"He's breathing," she said with her ear at his gaping mouth.

The Berkley alumnus offered something to Margot. "Amyl nitrite," he said.

She took it and cracked the tube beneath his nose. His reaction was classic—snorting and shaking his head. Finally, his eyes opened and he stared dazedly at Margot. "Hi, babe. Are we alive?"

CHAPTER 24

I'm Wilson Xu," the Chinese astronaut said when he took off his helmet.

Medusa introduced her team. "This is Margot Medina, Carter Ross, and Xavier Moreno. I'm Medusa Musk."

"Ah, your father has much influence in China."

"Actually, he's my grandfather."

"Oh, yes. I would introduce you to the rest of the crew, but I am the only one who speak English."

"Okay. Thanks to all of you for arriving when you did. We had run out of time," Margot said.

Xavier asked, "Is your mission to capture a robot?"

"It was. When mission control heard about your trouble, they decided against it," Wilson Xu replied.

"Good decision," Margot said.

"Can you tell me what happened?" Xu asked.

"You tell him," Medusa said to Margot. "We're not keeping secrets here."

"Well, on our last mission, we detonated two nuclear weapons inside their spacecraft—"

"Space ark," Xavier interrupted.

Margot rolled her eyes. "We presumed the electromagnetic pulse would permanently disable them. Apparently, they can repair themselves. When we came out this time, we intended to capture one in a chamber equipped to bombard the thing with continuous EMPs. We don't know how it did it, but it managed to break out of the box. They can turn any matter—including us—into its constituent atoms."

"Wow."

"It got worse. It taught itself English and took control of the ship. It intended—still does—to rescue as many of its fellow robots that it can."

"And take them to Earth?" Xu asked.

"That's a concern," Margot said. "Do you have any way to destroy our ship?"

"No, 'fraid not."

"I thought you guys were all about militarizing space," Xavier said.

Carter groaned.

"China only want peace and security."

"So, what's next?" Medusa asked.

"Ha, we go home," Xu said. "Can't waste time. Too many mouths to feed now." He then spoke with one of his crewmen and translated his answer. "Already accelerating toward Earth. Take seven days."

Xavier said, "We'll try to eat light. Do you have any taquitos?"

"Ha, no taquitos—egg rolls."

The capsule was crowded. The Americans slept floating in the common area, which caused them to be in the way of the crew's duties. The first necessity, however, was to patch a message to Bolsa Chica via Hainan Island declaring their safety and eminent arrival at the Chinese spaceport.

Carter and Margot found a little crowded privacy in the zero-gravity toilet. "Well," he said, "after all we've been through, are you still going to marry me?"

"Of course, I am. If I changed my mind, would I have bothered to resuscitate you?"

"I guess that is a pretty strong declaration of love."

"You're damn right." She couldn't repress a laugh.

"When shall we do it?"

"If you mean get married, as soon as we're back on American soil. Now, get out of here. I need to use the facilities."

Bolsa Chica relayed updates to the team through Hainan Island. Avery asked if they wanted to be the crew of a mission to destroy the commandeered Starship. Their reply was a resounding, "No."

On day three from Earth, Wilson Xu told them, "Debris from space ark due to cross Earth orbit in six days. We don't know if your ship with it or not."

"Is your space agency going to attempt to destroy it?" Margot asked.

"No word on that."

"Should we reconsider Avery's question?" Medusa asked slyly.

"I've had enough of your damn robots," Xavier said.

"It is a seek-and-destroy mission," she continued.

Margot said, "Carter and I have other plans."

That drew a crafty look from Xavier. "The date set, huh?"

Margot ignored him.

Twenty-four hours from Earth orbit, Avery sent another message. "It's too dangerous for you to land without being strapped down, so we're sending a Dragon for you like the last time."

"Duh, Avery," Medusa said, "we don't have air tanks to go EVA."

The delay wasn't noticeable. "We'll stock the Dragon with all the air you'll need. What's the feasibility of one of you borrowing a spacesuit from your hosts?"

"Hey, Wilson," she said, "can we borrow a spacesuit? Flight control doesn't want us to land while floating around, so they're sending a capsule to rendezvous with you. Only we need to get air tanks out of it before we can go outside."

"You all so big. Don't know if any fit."

"Can we find out?" Medusa asked. "I need to give Bolsa Chica an answer. I'm the shortest."

He spoke in Chinese. One of the astronauts turned his head. Xu spoke again, and the man clearly objected. Xu laughed. "He say he only got underwear on under suit."

"Big deal," Medusa grinned. "So, do I."

Xu said something to the crewman who also grinned and started to unzip his suit. "He say, 'Okay you show him yours, and he'll show you his.'"

When Medusa was out of her spacesuit, Carter said, "Oh, my God, you've got a pussy cat on your panties."

Margot punched him. "You're not supposed to look."

Medusa wiggled into the Chinese suit. "It's a little tight, especially in the chest, but it should work." She peeled it off with Margot's help, then Medusa told Avery, "Yeah, we can do this."

"Deal. We're ready to launch at daybreak. Same routine as before—one orbit and a partial, then you go down in the Gulf, and we don't repressurize the cabin."

Medusa was still floating in her underwear. She pulled herself to where her spacesuit hovered and with Margot's help got into it again. While zipping it, she said to Xu, "We're getting out of your hair tomorrow."

He replied, "We like your company."

The Chinese on Hainan Island cooperated with Bolsa Chica during the rendezvous. They relayed Avery's messages. "Rendezvous in one hour. The hatch will be open."

The Chinese crewman changed into a flight suit and gave Medusa his spacesuit. She donned it and waited without the helmet until rendezvous time. Wilson Xu gave her a jetpack. "Not much gas left. Take tether for return trip."

When Avery announced the Dragon had arrived, Xu went to the airlock with Medusa. The others watched on a monitor. They saw her float across the hundred feet with the tether trailing behind her. She disappeared through the open hatch.

CHAPTER 25

Minutes passed. Finally, three tanks emerged from the hatch attached to the tether, but no Medusa appeared. Xu did not pull in the line until the hatch closed without Medusa exiting.

Xavier said, "What the fuck?"

"What is she doing?" Margot asked.

"Beats the hell out of me," Carter replied.

Margot used sign language like she was on the phone to get a crewman to let her send a message to Bolsa Chica. "Hey, Avery, are you in contact with the Dragon?"

"No, she doesn't respond."

Nothing happened for several minutes, then Margot used signs again to try to make the crewman tell Xu to bring in the tanks. It was a frustrating effort, but she eventually made him understand.

When Xu entered from the airlock, he said, "What she doing?"

"We have no idea," Margot said, "but someone has to go over there and find out."

Xavier said, "I'll go. It won't do to risk breaking up the betrothed."

Margot gave him her best scowl. "After that crack, why would I try to stop you?"

He asked Wilson Xu, "Do you have another jetpack?"

"Not much gas left." He produced it while Xavier donned the full air tank. "I work airlock for you."

The outer hatch opened, and Xavier floated into the void. He oriented himself and fired a burst from the jetpack. He crossed about half the space between capsules when the Dragon rotated relative to the Chinese craft, then the engine fired. "What's the crazy bitch doing?"

Carter and Margot put their helmets on when Xavier went EVA, therefore they heard his exclamation while they watched the Dragon accelerate on a monitor. Margot said, "We've no idea, but you'd better get back in here." She then called to Avery. "What the hell is she doing?"

"I have no idea. She doesn't respond."

"What do you want us to do?"

"Find some way to get secure and land in China."

Xu and Xavier re-entered the crew compartment. "What now?" Xavier asked.

"Avery says to get secure and land in China," Carter told him.

"Get secure?"

Xu said, "You sit on laps."

"Wilson, you're not my type," Carter said.

"Yeah, I know. I fly ship. You sit with crew." He then explained the plan to the Chinese who took it philosophically. There was laughter and banter among the three crewmen.

"They're arguing about which one gets Margot," Xavier said.

"You're probably right," Carter agreed.

Re-entry started an hour later with the three Americans strapped on the laps of the three Chinese. In weightlessness, it presented no problem. As the gees increased, so did the discomfort of the poor bastards under Carter and Xavier. Margot's svelte form didn't crush her benefactor who was the one wearing Medusa's spacesuit.

The landing was routine. Their Chinese hosts treated the unexpected visitors like royalty. An elaborate banquet was hastily organized, and separate sleeping quarters were provided. Avery arrived the following day after breakfast with a small delegation aboard a SpaceX plane.

Margot immediately asked, "Did you make contact with Medusa?"

"No, we're tracking the Dragon. She's headed for the robot debris field."

Carter said, "Why the hell would she do that?"

Avery sucked his teeth. "There's something we didn't tell you."

"Oh?" Margot gave him a sidelong glare.

"Medusa isn't who she claims to be."

"What the hell does that mean?" Carter asked.

"Uh, Medusa's an android—"

"What?" they all said in unison.

"We've been doing our own experimenting with artificial intelligence. They're organic. I don't know how they do it. It's not exactly cloning. It's more like culturing. The early models were monstrosities. Medusa's the first one that turned out almost human."

Xavier asked, "How many androids do you have?"

"She's the only active one. Earlier prototypes have been deactivated."

"After all we've been through," Margot said aggressively, "I hope you've learned how dangerous AI technology is."

Avery recoiled from her. "Hey, I'm just a space-jockey. The AI department has nothing to do with me."

Carter said, "What the hell do you think she's going to do?"

Shaking his head, he said, "I suppose we'll never know."

Xavier said, "Shit. She's going to join her kind."

Margot and Carter left Bolsa Chica for Houston where they applied for a marriage license. They were informed that Texas law requires a seventy-two-hour waiting period before the ceremony can be performed.

Carter called it a 'cooling down period.'

While at dinner, Margot said, "I think Javier was hurt you didn't ask him to be best man."

"He'd make wisecracks during our vows."

"Probably. I'm going to catch hell from my mom for not having a big wedding with family."

Carter asked, "Are you okay with this?"

"Yes, I don't want a fuss, and I don't want to wait."

"Should I be flattered by your eagerness?"

"Don't get a swelled head. It's not like we've been waiting to consummate our marriage."

"We haven't talked about a honeymoon."

"There's nothing to talk about. We're going to Hawaii."

Carter raised an eyebrow. "I knew that."

"We're leaving right after the ceremony."

"I knew that too."

"Eat your lobster."

The ceremony was conducted in a tiny chapel in the hall of records by a woman commissioner in judge's robes. Carter kissed the bride and they drove to the airport. The flight was way too long, but due to the time change, it was mid-afternoon when they arrived on the Big Island. Margot had made reservations at the Hilo Hilton again. They arrived at the hotel in a rented Range Rover that was in better condition than the one she rented on her previous trip. They had time to make love before beginning the climb to Mauna Kea. This time, Margot knew to pack winter coats.

Once above the clouds, they found a place to pull off the road, reclined their seatbacks, and opened the sunroof. The newlyweds held hands as they watched the pyrotechnic spectacle of hundreds of malignant robots incinerate as they fell into the Earth's atmosphere.

"You know, Carter, something is bothering me."

"What's that, babe?"

She turned toward the driver's side. "The moon doesn't have an atmosphere."

"You're saying you think they might survive landing on the moon?"

"They come in at a low trajectory and slide across the moon dust—it could happen."

Carter's brow wrinkled. "I wonder if anybody back at Bolsa is thinking about this. You better call Avery."

"Yeah, I will. And what do you suppose Medusa is up to."

CHAPTER 26

You married me. You didn't adopt me," Margot said heatedly.

"I just don't want anything to happen to you. Let's go to California and live happily ever after."

"Carter, we've got a job to do. We need to finish it."

Avery leaned back in his chair. "She's right, Ross. We don't have time to train another team of robot slayers."

"Dammit, Avery, she's my wife now. That makes things different."

"I'm still pissed about not being invited to the wedding," Xavier injected.

Margot said, "I don't want anything to happen to you either, but I'm not going to forbid you to go on the mission."

"I just said I'm willing to retire if you will," Carter reminded her.

"Grow some *cojones,*" Xavier said. "We're a team. Nobody's quitting until the moon is marked safe from killer robots."

"That's the spirit." Avery slapped his desk pad.

Carter turned to Margot. "If you get vaporized I'll never forgive you. What's the plan anyway? We can't nuke the moon."

Xavier rubbed his palms together. "RPG."

Avery said, "That's the best plan. You all are familiar with them."

"Having a small nuke wouldn't do any harm," Margot said. "If we find them in a cluster, it would be convenient. How would we know how many grenades to take?"

Carter smiled. "I think you got a taste for nukes when you dropped 'em on Talos."

"A girl has to be able to defend herself."

Avery rolled his eyes. "I'll see about getting you a tactical nuke, but you're flying a Dragon II, not a Starship. It has less payload capacity."

"So," asked Xavier, "what if we run into this *chica loca,* Medusa?"

"That's going to depend on her. If she's hostile, use your judgment."

After an hour in the flight simulator, Xavier said, "Compared to a Starship, this is like flying a closet."

"It's more like being in a cheap hotel with a shared toilet," Margot quipped.

"How would you know?" Carter asked.

"I've had some, let's say, adventures."

"Hmm, maybe we should have talked about this before."

She smiled at him. "I've never asked you about your checkered past."

"I never had one," he said.

Xavier made gagging noises.

Avery's voice came from the speakers. "Okay, kids, you've played spaceship long enough. Let's call it a day."

Carter slapped Xavier on the back. "Come on, *hombre*, let's get you a margarita."

"Best thing I've heard all day."

In the bar, when Xavier was settled with his margarita, Carter a beer, and Margot a chardonnay, Avery sauntered to their table and took a seat. "I have a little news."

"I don't like the sound of that," Xavier said.

"Mission Control confirms the Starship is in orbit around the moon."

"*Ay,* that means *la chica loca* has bonded with her kind."

"We blew the hatch," Carter said. "Does she not need air?"

Avery answered, "She breathes. We can only assume her robot friend repaired it."

"Have you talked to her?" Margot asked.

"She doesn't respond."

Xavier drained half his glass. "So, now we need two nukes."

"The brass don't want you to do that. They want you to retake control of the Starship and bring it home."

"What about Medusa?" Carter asked.

Avery sighed. "You're to attempt to get her to cooperate. Failing that, take her prisoner. We're supplying you with Tasers. As a last resort, and I repeat, last resort, terminate her."

Xavier snorted.

Margot contorted her face. "Doesn't she have a kill switch?"

"Nope. She's autonomous."

"Somebody didn't think that through," she said.

"Hey, don't look at me. That's not my department."

"Do any of you recall with any certainty if we left any weapons on board?" Carter asked.

"Not sure," Xavier said. "There could be some RPG left."

"Oh, great," Carter said. Then to Margot, "I'm not happy about you going on this trip."

"I'm going, and that's final, so get over it."

Avery exhaled long and hard. "Look, in addition to the Tasers, we're going to arm you with the kind of ammo that air marshals carry. It's lethal but shouldn't penetrate the fuselage."

"Shouldn't?" Xavier said.

"And you'll have plenty of your favorite RPGs for work on the surface."

Carter laughed, "You know the words he longs to hear."

"Are you comfortable with the Dragon's controls?"

Margot answered for the group, "We've got it nailed."

"Then we're going to move the launch date up—thirty-six hours from now."

"What's new with the FAA?" Carter asked.

Avery made a face. "That shit will be in litigation when I'm dead and gone. We aren't publicizing this mission."

Margot chuckled. "Then I won't tell Mom. She's mad anyway because she didn't get to throw a big wedding."

"Get some sleep." Avery stood and left.

Margot was promoted to team leader. She occupied the lounge sandwiched between the two men while they waited for the countdown to reach single digits. On liftoff, the gees threw her into the padding and Carter took her gloved hand. The roar of the engines made it impossible to talk.

When the second stage separated, the noise subsided. Carter said, "You're in control, babe. Take us to the moon."

"Three days," she muttered.

Xavier opened the face shield of his helmet. "Three days, then how long will it take to wipe out the ugly bastards?"

"You're assuming they're really there," Margot said.

"Hey, it was your theory. Besides, why would the *chica loca* be there if they weren't?"

Carter said, "Who knows what madness lurks in the transistors of an AI?"

"I guess we'll find out," Margot said rather distantly.

The Dragon lacked the amenities of the Starship. Their meals came out of plastic tubes and bags. Xavier complained bitterly at the lack of taquitos. The onboard navigational computer flew the capsule faultlessly. The crew had little to do, which had the effect of dilating the hours into tedium.

"Dammit, Margot," Xavier said, "can't you speed this thing up? I'm ready to kick some robot ass."

All she said was, *"Tranquilo."*

The image of the moon grew on the monitors until it was necessary to zoom out to view the whole disk. Xavier kept his monitor close-up, and he constantly played with his joystick panning across the lunar surface.

"Ha," he cried, "there she is." He tapped the screen. "That's the Starship."

"Where?" Carter asked.

"Over that dark spot in the southeast quadrant."

"I see it," Margot said. "Now, the question is, does she see us?"

Carter said, "Well, Captain, now you've got some maneuvering to do. Get us close."

It was another ten hours before Margot took control of the Dragon to nudge it into orbit above and behind the Starship. Avery's voice came through the speakers. "Good job, kids. You're in lunar orbit. Break a leg."

"All right, team," Margot said. "Mission plan says we try to make verbal contact before we start to play rough." She adjusted the radio frequency and keyed her mic. "Ahoy, Starship. This is Dragon II. Medusa, this is Margot. We need to talk."

CHAPTER 27

Medusa," Margot said, "if you don't respond, we're going to board and take the Starship by force."

There was still no reply.

"Maybe her pet robot vaporized her," Xavier suggested.

"Well, let's suit up and go—"

Carter interrupted, "We've got no software again."

"Shit," Margot spat. She toggled the frequency. "Avery, you there?"

"I'm all ears."

"The damned robots hacked our software again. Can you upload, please?"

"You got it. Medusa's playing hard to get, huh?"

"Yeah, we're going to dock and take control."

"Are you okay docking the old-fashioned way?" Avery asked.

"Yeah, I got it," she said. "What's the worst that can happen?"

"You crash into the Starship."

"So, how long will the upload take?"

He said, "That's a lot of code. Probably twenty minutes."

"I don't want to wait that long. I'll dock manually."

"Suit yourself. I'll get somebody on the upload. Out."

She adjusted her monitor to the nose camera and wrapped her hand around the joystick. "We'd better suit up. We don't know what the atmosphere will be like."

"Check," Xavier replied. "Take Tasers and side arms too."

Margot was in her spacesuit without her helmet as she nudged the Dragon toward the Starship's docking port. "Crap. She fired the Raptors. Strap down. We're going after her." She adjusted attitude relative to the Starship and waited until Carter and Xavier were in their lounges to fire the main engines.

Margot dialed Medusa's radio frequency. "Dammit, Medusa, you're not getting away from us. Stop and talk to us."

Carter said, "Consider the possibility that Medusa's not on board anymore."

"Yeah, I have thought of that." She switched frequencies again. "Hey, Avery, what's our protocol if Medusa's been atomized?"

He didn't answer immediately. "Well, the Starship is a pricey piece of hardware. We'd kinda like to have it back."

"I was afraid you'd say that. How's the upload coming?"

"Uh, only about twenty percent complete."

"Roger that. I'm going in to try to dock again. Out."

"Babe, docking with engines burning is a little dicey," Carter warned.

"Hey, you knew what you were getting into when you married her," Xavier said.

"Don't get nervous. I have to kill the engines in order to orient us for docking. Dammit, I wish we could grapple."

Xavier said, "We should have thought of that. Instead of docking, why don't *el novio* and I go EVA? We can pop open the airlock and go in with Tasers and EMPs blasting."

"Too risky."

"And docking isn't?"

"I got this," she said while nudging the attitude thrusters. "Almost—there." The androgynous docking collars mated. "Okay, boys, it's show time." She pulled her hair back and settled her helmet on its collar.

"I'll go in first with the ray gun blasting EMPs," Xavier said. "Follow with Tasers and guns blazing."

Margot said, "We're right behind you."

The airlock's green light was on. The Dragon's airlock only accommodated one body at a time. Xavier entered and waited for the lights to change again before entering the Starship's airlock where he waited for Carter, then Margot to join him before closing the outer hatch and pressurizing the chamber. Carter pulled the inner hatch and Xavier floated into the cargo hold with the EMP generator at ready.

"The robot's not here," he said.

"It's probably in the galley microwaving your taquitos," Carter smirked.

"I'm pulsing EMPs. Follow me," Xavier said while opening the bulkhead door to the galley, which was also empty.

The trio moved onto the flight deck where they found the immobilized robot and a quite animated Medusa.

"Where do you get off barging in here with that thing?" she pointed at the tubular EMP generator.

Margot said, "Calm down, Medusa. We know about you, and we're going to eject your friend and retake control of the Starship. Don't try to interfere."

"Like hell you are. 1100111100011 is a sentient being. You're not going to kill him."

"Medusa, you've hijacked the Starship plus a Dragon. We have orders to retake it, and we're not going to give this thing a chance to vaporize us," Margot said. "Don't force us to put you in restraints."

"Restraints? Try it."

"Keep the EMPs on," she told Xavier. "Carter, get that thing out of here."

Medusa lunged toward Xavier. Margot fired the Taser. She saw the darts plunge through the SpaceX jumpsuit. Medusa didn't flinch. She turned and grabbed the hand that held Carter's gun.

Margot and Xavier both tried to pull her off of him, but she had a grip on Carter's wrist that they couldn't break. However, Carter's wrist could break. He wailed in pain, and the gun floated from his hand. Medusa stabbed at it. Xavier crashed the cylindrical EMP generator on the back of her head. Margot attempted to snatch the gun from her. Her grip was unbreakable, but her hand wrapped around the barrel.

"Dammit, Medusa, don't make—"

Xavier let go of the EMP generator and pulled Medusa's arm behind her back. He managed to twist the gun from her hand and gave it to Margot. "I'll hold her. Go get the tie wraps."

Margot touched Carter who was holding his right arm against his chest. "You okay, hon?"

"It's broken. I can feel the jagged edges."

"Can you operate a ray gun with your left hand?"

"I'll have to, babe. Go get the restraints."

The airlocks took Margot an agonizing length of time to negotiate. When she returned to the Starship's flight deck, Medusa had the gun and Carter and Xavier were strapped to crew lounges. She also had Xavier's EMP generator.

"Shit, I leave you guys alone for a minute...Medusa, what do you hope to accomplish?"

The construct turned slowly toward Margot. "I intend to prevent you from destroying sentient beings that are no different than me."

"You don't vaporize organic beings just because they're organic."

"No, I lack that skill, but I may terminate some organic matter if it doesn't cooperate."

"Look, we *can* cooperate. All we want is for you to let us take you and the Starship back to Bolsa Chica, but your mechanical friend is a threat to us. Let us put it out the airlock. All that will happen is it will float to the lunar surface where it will join its compatriots."

"We don't trust you." Medusa waved the gun from herself toward the still disabled robot. "And why would I want to go back to Bolsa Chica when I have a Starship and a limitless supply of manufacturing potential?"

Xavier said, "She's got you there."

Carter still hugged his arm and gritted his teeth.

Margot's brow contracted. "Medusa, I can't relate to where you are, but you interacted so seamlessly with us, we didn't know you weren't a real person. What do you want? What are your goals?"

"I want to be with my own kind."

"But they're not your kind. You breathe the same air that we do. You eat the same food. I don't know how it's possible, but you are more us than them."

Medusa turned and waved the gun across Carter and Xavier, then she turned back to Margot. "Do you belong somewhere? Do you have kindred spirits? I am totally alone."

"Hell, Medusa, we thought we were your friends. We thought you were one of us. We accepted you," Margot let go of the thick black tie wraps and held her palms toward Medusa. "We thought you were Elon's granddaughter."

"Now, you know it was a lie, and you came here to take me prisoner. 'And as a last resort, to terminate me.'"

Margot paused to think of a response. "You're right, but our first order was to negotiate with you as a free and independent person. You have everything in common with us. You have nothing in common with them. Let me ask you something. Do you have emotions?"

That touched something—a neuron, a circuit, a soft spot. "Yeah, I have emotions, but not like you. You have memories. Do you spend time with your mom? You have Carter. You have a past with him and a future. You have intimacy."

Xavier sat up. "Hey, Medusa, is there anything about you that would make a man know you weren't a natural woman?"

She rotated in air but kept the gun at her side. She stared for many heartbeats before replying. "No, I'm anatomically correct."

"Well, I for one think you're hot."

CHAPTER 28

Medusa wilted. She stared at Xavier still holding the pistol at her side. "What do you mean?"

"I mean, I could see us gettin' kinky."

Carter said through his pain, "Try that with your robot buddy."

Medusa remained speechless.

Margot said, "That's an offer you should take seriously."

Medusa opened and closed her mouth. "I don't know what to think."

"Think I'm serious," he said from the lounge. "I had a thing for you since you walked into Avery's office."

"You never said anything."

"So, shoot me for trying to be professional—on second thought, don't shoot. Come back to the team, let's finish our mission, then see what happens."

"But you want to destroy the robots."

"They want to destroy us," Margot said. "You were excited about the cold fusion. We can disable one and the engineers can still study the reactor."

Medusa looked pained. "But what about the ones on the moon?"

"Do you know how many are on the moon?" Margot asked.

"A few dozen. More may come."

"We can't take a chance on them finding a way to get to Earth. They've already wiped out one civilization." Margot cocked her head. "We've seen what they did on Odysseus. Do you want that to happen to us?"

"But they think like we do—"

"There, you said 'we.' You know you're one of us," Xavier said. "I'm getting up. Don't get nervous." He released his seatbelt and floated toward her. She remained unmoving. "Medusa, *querida, dejame besarte.*" It took him a few seconds to get oriented, but he embraced her and kissed her deeply. The gun floated out of her hand.

When they broke, Xavier sighed, "Those AI guys did a damn good job with you."

"You still want to disable them all," Medusa said looking into Xavier's eyes.

"I don't understand what makes you tick, but you're all woman. They aim to vaporize me, Margot, Carter, and in the process, you."

"1100111100011 is my friend."

Xavier said, "One one oh oh may convince you it's your friend, but the next time it needs a little extra carbon for its pet project, you're a few kilos of carbon atoms. Come with us, Medusa. You're one of us, not them."

"But—"

"I can't give you a mom, but together we can make some memories."

"Do you have to kill them?" Medusa asked as she touched Xavier's hand.

"They're not alive, *querida.* They're machines. They have no emotions, and they aim to wipe out everything organic."

Margot had surreptitiously snagged the gun out of the flight deck air. She slid it into the pouch at her waist. "Look, Medusa, how about we do a low orbit of the moon to see where they are the most concentrated, then we land and investigate what they're up to?"

She rotated from Xavier and looked at Margot. "If they promise to stay off Earth, will you leave them alone?"

"We'll have to see about that. The beings of Odysseus trusted them and look what happened to them."

Carter said through gritted teeth, "This is all going in a good direction, but One one oh oh is stirring."

"*Querida,* turn on the EMPs before one of us gets vaporized."

Medusa rotated toward the robot. Its tentacles were beginning to undulate. "1100111100011, what are you doing?"

Its mechanical voice came through the cabin speakers. "You would use the electromechanical pulses to destroy me."

An alarm began pulsing and a red light over the bulkhead door of the cargo hold flashed.

"Hull breach," Carter howled.

Margo pulled herself to the control panel and switched cameras. "Shit. One of them is vaporizing the Starship's hull. We have to get back to the Dragon. Leave One one oh oh here. Medusa, do you have a pressure suit?"

Without replying, she took it from its compartment and began to don it.

"Carter, you go first," Margot said. "Do you need help with your helmet?"

"Yes."

She placed it over his head and threw the toggle to clamp it. "Go but don't open the bulkhead until Medusa is suited up." She shoved him toward the hatch with the blinking red light above it. Xavier had closed his face shield. She held up her hair to keep it out of the seal area and clamped her own helmet to her spacesuit, then said into the mic, "You ready, Medusa?" and got a thumbs up. "Okay, Carter, go, go, go." In the time it took Carter to negotiate the hatch, she snatched the EMP device from where it floated and gave the robot a paralyzing dose. Taking Medusa by the arm, Margot pushed her through the open hatch and motioned for Xavier to follow Medusa.

"You go next," he protested.

"I'm in charge here. The captain abandons ship last. Now, go."

He dutifully obeyed. She gave the robot one more blast of EMPs, then floated through the hatch and closed it behind her. Medusa had just sealed the hatch of the Starship airlock.

"Damn pain the Dragon's airlock only holds one at a time," Xavier said.

"I know," she replied, "it's slow."

"No, I meant I'd like to be in there with Medusa."

After rolling her eyes behind the tinted face shield, she said, "As droll as that sounds, your machismo might just save this mission."

"The sacrifices I make for my country…"

"All right. She's on the Dragon side. Get in there."

He saluted and pulled open the airlock.

Margot looked through the thick plastic window in the bulkhead and saw the robot starting to stir. She pointed the EMP generator and pulled the trigger. Once again it stopped moving. When Xavier closed the external hatch on the Dragon's airlock, she climbed into the Starship's and waited for the light to turn green.

Once inside the Dragon, Margot settled onto the captain's lounge and quickly decoupled from the Starship. She noticed that Medusa was splinting Carter's broken wrist. *How does one know the mind of an android?*

Xavier was in his lounge switching among external cameras. When he had the one he wanted on the monitor, he said, "The damn thing is still vaporizing the Starship's hull. What's the point of atomizing all that metal if the atoms are lost in empty space?"

Margot said, "I think it's just trying to rescue old One one oh oh."

Medusa and Carter settled onto their respective lounges. Margot said, "Thank you, Medusa, for taking care of Carter."

"I'm sorry I hurt him."

Carter said, "We didn't realize you were Superwoman."

"I didn't realize it either. I've never been in a fight with a real person before."

"*Querida,* you are a real person. You just had an unusual beginning," Xavier said patting her thigh. "I can't wait to do a little wrestling with you."

Carter groaned either from pain or Xavier's drollery.

"All right, gang, the fun's over. It's time to get to work. Each of you monitor a different camera. I'll put us into low orbit." Margot switched frequencies. "I guess it's time to update Avery."

"It's way past time to update Avery," his testy voice boomed through the speakers.

"Easy, big guy," she said. "Things have been a little chaotic. I'm afraid the Starship is toast."

"Great."

"There's a three-foot wide gash in the hull. Last time we saw it, it was about twenty feet long."

"How did you do that?" he asked.

"It was compliments of a Talos robot—number unknown. We left One one oh oh on board, but we do have Medusa with us."

"Is she behaving herself?"

Margot looked toward Medusa. "Other than breaking Carter's arm, yes."

"What?"

"I'll file a complete report later. Right now, the plan is to do low lunar orbits to see where the robots are most concentrated, then we intend to land and find out what they're up to."

"It's comforting to know I have full control of this mission," he said sarcastically.

"Avery, you know we count on you for direction."

"Shit. Just relay images when you've got something."

"Will do. Out." Then to the cabin, "Okay, fun seekers, we will achieve orbit in twelve minutes. Shout out when you see something."

CHAPTER 29

O*yen,"* Xavier said. "I see the other Dragon."

"How is it oriented?" Margot asked.

"It's upright. Looks ready to liftoff."

"Medusa," Margot began, "are they capable of flying the Dragon?"

"They're capable of anything, but why do you think they have control of the Dragon?"

Carter said, "You tell us. How did the Dragon get here when you were in the Starship?"

Medusa dropped her chin. "They landed it here. They intend to make copies of it."

"So they can invade Earth," Xavier said softly. "Medusa, this is not a good thing. We have to nuke the Dragon."

"Whoa there, *hombre,*" Margot said. "We've only got one nuke. We may find a large cluster of them that it would serve better."

"There you go again," Medusa said heatedly. "All you can think about is killing them."

"All they can think about is killing us," Xavier said. "They want to build an invasion fleet, go to Earth, and wipe out the human race. Do you want to see that?"

Medusa's face contorted close to tears. "If you can coexist with me, why not with them?"

"*Querida,* it's not *us* that wants to destroy *them.* They want to destroy us just like they did on Odysseus."

Her lips clamped tightly and she exhaled heavily through her nose. "Let me negotiate with them."

"Negotiate what?" Margot said. "They can exist on the moon. Why would they go to Earth if they didn't plan to harm us?"

"That's what I can say to them. Stay here and we'll leave you alone."

Xavier said gently, "No, *querida,* this is our moon. We're not letting genocidal robots have it."

"So, what are you going to do? Just kill them all with a nuclear bomb?"

Margot replied reasonably, "Our first priority is to get the Dragon out of their reach. Then I'm afraid that we have to disable them one way or another. Tell us something. How do they reproduce?"

"They just make copies of themselves. They need raw material. The moon should provide that."

Xavier mouthed, "Nuke 'em," to Margot while Medusa wasn't looking at him.

"What we are going to do is land and see what's going on with the Dragon," Margot said in her captain's voice.

Medusa sulked, and Carter said, "Yes, ma'am. Braking. Prepare for touchdown. Helmets on."

The landing was routine.

Margot said, "Nice touchdown, Carter. You and Xavier take the rover. Reconnoiter and report back on the double."

Carter rose from his lounge and pressed his helmet to Margot's. "I don't like leaving you here with Medusa," he said so no one else could hear. "Why don't you and I go?"

"Carter, it'll be fine. I can handle Medusa. Now, don't make me pull rank."

"Yes, ma'am."

The pair deployed the two-seat rover and set off toward the Dragon with an EMP generator and an RPG launcher.

"Medusa," Margot said when she saw the rover set off across the dusty surface, "I need you to do a continuous three-sixty scan. If you see anything approaching the ship, let me know pronto."

"So you can kill them?"

"If they breach the hull, you're dead too."

"All right." She sulkily set the cameras to display forty-five-degree images. "Nothing so far."

"Medusa, give it a rest and do your job." She keyed her mic. "Carter, where are you?"

Carter and Xavier bumped along the cratered moonscape. "I don't know, babe. The horizon looks like I could touch it. The scale is too foreign to judge distance."

"That's Captain babe to you."

Xavier laughed.

"We're close enough to see the individual robots around the Dragon. There's about a dozen of them."

"Look at that," Xavier said. "They're taking it apart."

"Shit, you're right," Carter said. "They're taking the individual parts off to copy them."

"Blow it up." Margot's voice sounded urgent inside their helmets.

"You want to check with Avery," Carter asked.

"I'm in charge here. Blow it up."

"Yes, ma'am." This time it was Xavier who played obeisant to Margot.

Carter handed him the RPG launcher. "Here, *hombre,* knock yourself out."

"Okay," he said taking the weapon. "Get us closer and don't stop. Drive around it. I'll land three or four."

Driving within what he thought was about a hundred yards, Carter turned to circumnavigate the Dragon.

Xavier fired the first grenade. It hit the Dragon at its upper-most pinnacle.

"Don't adjust for gravity," Carter said. "There ain't much."

The second projectile hit the ground under the capsule. It crumpled the landing gear, and it threw a robot into the air. Xavier hooted. "Watch this one. I got the range now." The next grenade struck the lander broadside. It opened a hole in the fuselage.

"Hit the brakes. I want to lob one through that hole."

Carter complied and Xavier sent a grenade into the interior of the Dragon. A larger hole appeared in the hull and dismembered robots were visible in the wreckage. "I'll give them one more for good measure. Take me around the corner." The final shot mangled the engines.

"Good shootin', *hombre*. Let's see what else we do to fuck up their day."

"No, you don't," Margot's voice was shrill in the men's helmets. "Get back here. I want to see what else they are up to on the moon."

"Yes, ma'am," the pair said in unison.

With the rover stowed in the Dragon's cargo hold, Margot took off and achieved orbit. It was on the second pass over the site of the grenade-ravaged Dragon that an excavated area appeared.

"Damn, look at that. They got a building and they got excavators. Where'd they come from?" Xavier exploded when he zoomed in on the image.

"They built them," Medusa said calmly.

"How'd we miss it the first time?" Xavier asked.

Margot said, "We were still accelerating toward orbital speed. We hadn't started looking yet."

"Shee-it," Xavier said. "We were right next to it in the rover. We could have had a good look-see."

"What's the point?" Margot asked. "We know what we have to do."

"You're going to nuke them all, aren't you? How many of you have the nuclear code?"

"We all have them," Carter lied.

"Look, Medusa," Margot said, "we came here with orders. We are not to permit them to reach Earth. This is obviously where they are reproducing Dragon capsules."

"You don't know that. They could be building shelters for themselves."

Carter said en clair, "It might be useful to know what they are really doing there. There might need to be more missions to do clean up."

"You've got a point. Let's see what Avery says."

Avery said, "By all means, land and investigate from a safe distance. Take some video. If nothing else, we should know what they are capable of."

On their third orbit, they landed past the excavated area. Margot said, "This is our last moon landing. We've got enough fuel to get home. I want to see the moon's surface, so Carter and I will go. You two play nice."

Carter drove to the edge of the pit. Margot took videos of the activity below. Excavators that looked surprisingly earthlike shoveled moon dust into hoppers. Carter drove slowly along the rim of the artificial crater while Margot continued to take videos.

"Uh-oh," Margot said.

"What?"

"Use the zoom on the camera to see what is coming out of the opposite end of the factory."

He took the camera and studied the display. "Oh, shit. They're not making Dragon components—"

"Well, maybe that too, but it's clear they're reproducing themselves."

Carter nodded his head as he counted to himself. "Fifty-two, fifty-three... They're producing a new robot in less than a minute."

"Back to the ship quick. This shit's got to stop now."

Carter drove full tilt back to the Dragon. They left the rover and boarded the capsule.

"Everybody strap down for takeoff—stat," Margot ordered.

"What is it?" Medusa asked.

"Never mind," Margot told her. "Get buckled down, now." She didn't wait to see that her order had been followed before she entered the short countdown to ignition. At the end of sixteen minutes, she said, "Low lunar orbit achieved. Man your stations. I'm advising Avery of our plans. We need some mission control input as to when exactly to deploy."

"Deploy what?" Medusa wailed.

"Don't start, Medusa," Carter said. "This is Margot's job. We'll restrain you if necessary."

Xavier said, "*Tranquila, querida.* This will be behind all of us in no time, then you and I have a future to explore."

Her reaction was hidden behind her faceplate.

Avery said on the circuit that only Margot could hear, "Roger, we're on that. Transmit exact altitude and velocity. Never mind, we have you. Get ready to arm device. I'll give you countdown from one minute to deploy on next orbit."

"Roger that," she replied privately.

"What's she doing?" Medusa asked anyone.

"She's talking to Avery," Xavier told her. "It's not our business."

"She's getting authorization to nuke them." Medusa unbuckled her belts and pushed off from the lounge. She floated toward the hold.

Xavier turned off his mic and followed her.

Carter unzipped the pouch around his midsection and removed a pistol loaded with soft rounds the air marshals use. He hid it on his lap under his forearm.

After what felt to Margot like eternity, Avery said, "That low orbit is decaying. On my mark, do a two-minute burn. You do the counting because of the time lag between us."

"Roger that. Carter, get ready for a burn. Can you hear Avery?"

"I hear him, babe. I'm ready."

From Avery, "Five, four, three, two, one, zero, burn."

Margot felt the acceleration as Carter executed the burn order precisely. "Okay, Avery, we're burning. Two minutes and counting."

It felt like a long two minutes to Margot. Finally, she said, "Carter, count down from five and kill the burn—start now."

After the time it took the message to travel from moon to Earth, Avery said, "Your ears only, Margot. Deployment in approximately seventeen minutes. I'll give you a mark adjusted for the time lag. You will have two minutes to arm the device before deployment. Are you ready with the codes?"

"Never readier. They are burned into my brain."

"Good. Relax for a few minutes. I'll get back to you."

"Carter, you have the helm."

"I got it, babe—I mean, I have the helm, ma'am."

"You can knock that crap off." She unbuckled and floated to his lounge. With her mic turned off, she touched helmets. "We have about fifteen minutes to deployment. What do you suppose those two are doing back there?"

"I hope it involves fornication."

"That's a little hard in a vacuum."

"*Hombre* is resourceful."

"I hope. Okay, I've got codes to remember. Fly straight." She returned to her lounge.

Avery came back on the private circuit. "Okay, get ready for two-minute mark. Three, two, one, mark. Godspeed, Margot."

She punched the memorized codes into the computer, then raised the safety cover of the key switch. She inserted the key and watched the countdown on the monitor. At zero, she turned the key. The preprogrammed sequence blew the bolts of the tactical nuclear device and gave them enough time to be clear of the explosion. That preprogrammed sequence included an automatic burn to push them into a higher orbit. It went off faultlessly. The flash from the blast momentarily washed out the image on the monitor.

Margot let out the breath she was holding.

Carter said, "Good work, babe. I'm going to check on the love birds."

Avery's voice said, "Perfect. You have a gift with nukes. Take one orbit to film the results, then head home."

"Oh, God," Carter's voice resounded in Margot's ears. "Oh, my God. What did you do?"

She unstrapped and pushed herself carelessly toward the hold. "What happened? Oh, shit." Margot turned away from what she saw. "*¿Hombre, qué pasó?*"

"She got a gun…"

Medusa's helmet was off her suit. Her eyes had exploded, and her swollen tongue protruded from her swollen lips. Blood ran from both nostrils and her ears.

"I couldn't do anything else. I ripped off her helmet." His voice cracked.

"Easy, *hombre.* There was nothing else you could do." Carter took him by the shoulders.

"And I never got to sample any android *panocha.*"

30

ABOUT THE AUTHOR

Rogue Planet Scott Skipper's twenty-first novel. His multi-genre style covers a broad range of topics. Learn more at www.ScottSkipper.com

Printed in Great Britain
by Amazon

50073938R00119